3/06

the
SACRIFICE

the
SACRIFICE

KATHLEEN BENNER DUBLE

Margaret K. McElderry Books
New York London Toronto Sydney

Margaret K. McElderry Books • An imprint of Simon & Schuster Children's Publishing Division 1230 Avenue of the Americas, New York, New York 10020 • This book is a work of fiction. Any references to historical events, real people, or real locales are used fictitiously. Other names, characters, places, and incidents are products of the author's imagination, and any resemblance to actual events or locales or persons, living or dead, is entirely coincidental. •
Book design by Sonia Chaghatzbanian • The text for this book is set in Adobe Garamond. • Manufactured in the United States of America • 10 9 8 7 6 5 4 3 2 1 • Library of Congress Cataloging-in-Publication Data • Duble, Kathleen Benner. • The sacrifice / Kathleen Benner Duble.—1st ed. • p. cm. • Summary: Two sisters, aged ten and twelve, are accused of witchcraft in Andover, Massachusetts, in 1692 and await trial in a miserable prison while their mother desperately searches for some way to obtain their freedom. • ISBN-13: 978-0-689-87650-9 ISBN-10: 0-689-87650-5 (hardcover) • [1. Mothers and daughters—Fiction. 2. Sisters—Fiction. 3. Witchcraft—Fiction. 4. Puritans—Fiction. 5. Family life—Massachusetts—Fiction. 6. Massachusetts—History—Colonial period, ca. 1600–1775—Fiction.] I. Title.
PZ7.D8496Sac 2005 • [Fic]—dc22 • 2004018355

FIRST
EDITION

*For my father, who gave me the inspiration,
and my mother, who taught me the determination*

acknowledgments

No work is ever the effort of a single individual. In the case of the story of Abigail Faulkner and her family, I have had many people add their insights, knowledge, and creativity to the process.

I would first like to thank the Society of Children's Book Writers and Illustrators for recognizing the potential in this unfinished manuscript by naming it a Work-in-Progress runner-up, and in rewarding that potential monetarily. The money was welcome; the recognition, a true gift.

Because I am a writer and not a historian, to Juliet H. Mofford of the Andover Historical Society, I thank you for giving your time to read my manuscript and sharing your expert opinion.

To Liz Fredrick, Donna McArdle, and Marcia Strykowski, thanks for your attentive ears, warm praise, and heartfelt criticism. Your critiques are invaluable, not just to this manuscript, but to everything I write.

To Amy Hourihan and Jenny Steward, thanks for

lending your keen eye, sharp wit, and abundant intelligence to the proofing of my galleys, a tedious task for which I am most grateful.

To my daughter Tobey, thanks for taking time out of your crazy high-school schedule to wander the graveyard in North Andover for a decent photo of your mother. I know this took some time!

To my daughter Liza, thanks for making me laugh. I hope you'll read *this* book.

To my husband, Chris, thanks for the time you put into reading draft after draft of my manuscripts and galleys. You always seem to be able to pinpoint where I've gone wrong. I look forward to the day when you can tell me how to fix it.

To my editor, Sarah Sevier, who, thankfully, does know how to fix it: You took on this manuscript, directed me clearly and concisely, and tightened and strengthened the story with a skill I can only try some day to replicate.

And finally, to my father, who found the story in the first place: I thank you for always doing the grunt work on so many things for me, whether it is researching the best computer for our family, flying across the country to help me in a crisis, or finding me an ancestor with a story I was destined to tell. You're the best!

the
SACRIFICE

one

"They will not see me move.
They will not see me move," Abigail whispered to
herself, although her whole body cried out to shift
her legs and ease the pain as she sat straight and still
in the stocks. Her legs burned and her backside
ached, but she remained determined. She kept her
head held high, even when a cold mist developed,
sending shivers through her body. Even when her
cousin Steven, who had teased her into lifting her
skirts and racing him in the first place, came and
grinned at her. Even when Goody Sprague walked
past and stared at her with disdain. Abigail did not
move. She did not even blink an eye. She wouldn't.

Abby did not for an instant believe it was evil for
a girl to take pleasure in running and having her legs

free. If she wasn't meant to race, why had the Lord given her those legs in the first place?

Her right thigh begin to twitch. She tightened the muscles with all her might and gritted her teeth.

"They will not see me move. They will not see me move," she continued to whisper to herself.

Rain was now dribbling down her back, snaking its way between her shoulder blades, cold and wet. Abby sat up straighter.

The parchment paper sign, SINNER, that hung about her neck grew damp and clung to her bodice. Cold crept into her hands, which lay clasped in her lap. With her feet locked into place and her legs stretched straight out in front of her with no support, Abby felt strained beyond enduring. She willed herself to see her limbs in the wooden holes as if they were someone else's, removed from the pain.

It felt as if days had passed, though Abigail knew her sentence was only six hours. She was hungry, yet this made her more determined. She lifted her head higher and peered out into the growing darkness, watching lights appear as each house in the village lit its candles.

At last, just when she felt as if she couldn't stand

it any longer, they came: four of the town elders and Abigail's grandfather, Reverend Dane.

Abigail looked straight into Grandpappy's eyes. She regretted having shamed him, but she was not sorry for the racing. Surely he had mistaken the words of the Lord if he believed that she was a sinner. Abby knew that she flew like the angels when she ran.

"Your punishment is complete, Abigail Faulkner," Justice Bradstreet said. "Release her."

The others lifted the bar of the stocks. Abby stared at the men, and left her legs there. She would not move until they had left. She was not about to let them see her shake and perhaps fall as she attempted to stand on her stiff and weak legs.

"Are you not yet repentant, Abigail?" asked Elder Stevens in wonder.

Abby saw Grandpappy's face turn scarlet at her refusal to move. She knew he would not like how she was about to answer Elder Stevens. Abigail thrust forth her chin and prepared to speak.

But she was saved from saying anything by the arrival of her mother. Mama came from the shadows and descended upon them, her face stern and drawn.

"Please, good sirs, leave me to tend to her," she

said. "The child will sicken if we leave her here much longer. Can you not discuss saving her soul in more tolerable weather? Let me take her home now."

The elders grumbled but finally turned and left for their own homes, warm fires, and suppers.

"You are too easy on her, Hannah," Grandpappy said.

"Not now, Father," Mama said. "We can discuss this at a later time."

Grandpappy grunted. He gave Abby one last look, then headed off into the darkness.

Mama turned toward her daughter. Her eyes searched Abigail's, but she said nothing. Quickly, she leaned down and began to rub Abby's legs until Abby began to feel them again. The sensation was painful, and Abigail had to bite her lip to stop from crying out.

Mama leaned over and put her arms around her daughter. "Can you move your legs?"

Abigail lifted first one leg, and then the other to the ground. Pain tore through each one as she moved them from the stocks.

"I fear I may not make it home, Mama," she whispered.

Mama lifted Abigail slightly. "I'll wager you'll do it, Bear. But rise slowly now."

At the sound of Mama's nickname for her, Abby blinked back tears. She remembered the day her mother had first called her that. She was only five years old, and a big black bear had wandered into their garden. Abigail had just finished her daily weeding when she saw the bear rooting around, tearing up the garden she had just put in order.

"Get out of here!" Abigail had yelled, bringing her mother to the door.

"Abby," her mother had said softly, gesturing furiously at her. "Come slowly here, child. Back away from him."

"I will not," Abby had replied angrily, picking up a stick. "Get out, you old bear!"

"Abigail, stop," her mother whispered. "You'll make him angry."

But Abigail would not stop. She banged that stick against the wooden gate of the garden, attracting the bear's attention, then moved slowly toward him. She hit the stick again, continuing to move toward the bear and the garden gate. Finally, the bear backed away, then fled into the woods.

"Abby," her mother said, running forward and clutching her daughter to her. "Are you mad? Don't you ever do that again!"

"I will," Abby had said fiercely. "I'm not about to hoe this garden twice for any old bear."

Her mother had laughed and kissed her daughter. "You are fierce enough to be part bear yourself, child," she had said.

Thinking of this memory, Abigail willed herself to be courageous now. But her legs ached terribly, and the tears threatened.

"Steady," Mama whispered. "'Tis not seemly to cry here, Abigail. Let us get you back home. You have withstood this most bravely. Do not let them see you weaken now."

Abby nodded and began to take her first steps, leaning upon her mother. Her legs shook and her feet felt numb, but she felt more confident with Mama's arm strong and sure around her.

"Slowly, Abigail," Mama whispered.

Abby did not glance up at the steep climb ahead of them to their home. Instead, she looked down at the muddy road, concentrating on every step, placing each foot carefully before adding weight to it. Slowly they walked up the hill until at last, Mama stopped.

"We're home, Bear," Mama said. "Dorothy!" she called.

The door swung open, and Abigail sighed with relief at the sight of her sweet home stretched out in front of her. She took the last few steps inside and collapsed onto a stool, weak and weary.

She had made it. She was home.

"Drink this," Mama said, handing Abby a warm mug of steaming cider.

Abigail, who lay in bed with several coverlets over her, took the pewter mug and drank deeply. The warmth of the cider ran through her. Still, she shivered.

Outside, the night watch called the hour.

"Take your ease, Bear," Mama whispered. "I want you abed this evening. Tomorrow is the Sabbath, and you'll be wanted at the service. So rest now."

Abby scowled. Already, she could feel the stares of the congregation and the fiery sermon her grandfather would deliver for her benefit alone. She could feel the aches in her bones as she tried to sit still for the four hours of service on the hard wooden pew of the meetinghouse. After a day in the stocks, she knew this would be no easy task. It angered her to think that she would have to withstand a long sermon on top of today's punishment.

Mama smiled and stroked Abigail's cheek. "Stop fussing, Abby. You'll face tomorrow bravely. You proved today that you're stouthearted enough."

"Mama, what Abby did was wrong," Dorothy whispered. Abigail's older sister stood at the door with a bowl of stew and a piece of corn bread.

Abigail could smell the stew, and her mouth watered.

"Dorothy, come," Mama said. "Bring Abigail's food here and take her soiled garments downstairs with you."

"But Mama," Dorothy continued, as she handed the bowl to Abigail, "it's wrong for her to race. Shouldn't we be telling her not to do it?"

Mama sighed and reached out to rest her hand on top of Dorothy's head. "I know they say it is wrong, daughter, but I fear I am as uncertain as your sister as to why lifting one's skirts and racing is against the Lord."

"It's sinful, Mama," Dorothy said. She turned

and looked at her ten-year-old sister. "I fear for Abigail's soul."

Mama laughed. "It seems anything that is pleasurable is sinful, dear one, and as for Abby's soul, she is as innocent as you are. Do not take things so seriously, Dorothy. Life is hard enough without some joy at times. Perhaps I shall have you join Abigail here, and let you race with the devil for a fortnight."

"Mama!" Dorothy said, her eyes wide.

Mama laughed again.

Then Dorothy, too, began to laugh. "I would never race, Mama," Dorothy said, making a face, "as I do most truly hate to run."

Mama and Dorothy laughed all the harder. Mama hugged Dorothy and then gave her a little push. "Take the garments, Dorothy. We will speak more on this matter later. Tonight I am weary, as is Abigail."

"Are you all right, Abby?" Dorothy asked, turning to her sister.

"Aye," Abigail answered with a weak smile. "I shall be fine on the morrow."

Dorothy picked up the wet clothes and left the room, looking back uncertainly at Mama and Abigail.

"So, daughter, pray, tell me. Was the race worth the result?" Mama asked.

Abigail swallowed her stew before answering. She was well aware of what her family would suffer because of her behavior. But then she thought of the run, of the race across the field this morning, of the way she'd let her legs fly. *It was worth it,* she thought fiercely. *It was worth every minute.*

"Say it not, Bear," Mama said, smiling. "I see the answer in your face."

Then Mama's smile dimmed. "Still, I fear life will not be easy for you should you always insist on doing things in your own fashion." She rose from the feather mattress, taking the bowl from Abigail's hand.

"Mama," Abby said, "I am sorry for the trouble I cause you."

Mama bent and kissed her daughter. She stroked her cheek. "Oh, Abby," she said. "I truly don't mind if it means you are happy."

There was a noise in the doorway. Abby's father was there, shuffling back and forth. He cleared his throat as he shifted from foot to foot. "How fare you, Abigail?" he asked, not looking at her.

"Well," she replied. Her impatience rose at the

sight of him. He had not come to check on her once while she was in the stocks. She had known he wouldn't. He never could face anything unpleasant, and that fact irritated Abby.

Her father nodded. "All right, then."

He turned and was gone.

Abby's mother sighed. "If only happiness for others in this house could be so easily won," she said.

Abigail knew Mama loved Papa, and so she understood her mother's sadness. Abby loved him too, but she hated his weakness and sometimes lost patience with him, even when she tried her hardest not to.

"Good night, Abigail," Mama whispered, then blew out the candle in the room.

"Good night, Mama," Abigail whispered back. She turned on her side and stared into the darkness. Her legs ached from having been held so straight and stiff in the stocks. She knew the pain would keep her from sleep. And too, Abby wished tomorrow was any day but the Sabbath.

two

Abigail woke to find her body stiff and sore. She moaned slightly as she turned over in bed. Even the feathers beneath her seemed to poke at every weary spot on her body. In the room next door, Abby could hear Mama and Papa talking, and she noticed that Dorothy was not in bed with her. Mama had obviously let her sleep later than normal on the Sabbath, and Abigail was grateful for that, but now she must hurry in order to be ready in time.

Painfully, she pushed herself up and out of bed. Her legs wobbled beneath her, and she grabbed onto the washstand to steady herself.

She used the chamber pot and then washed her face and hands. The water was bitingly cold, and

Abigail wished she could go back to her bed and coverlets. But staying in bed was not possible. She must sit through the long Sabbath service, like it or not.

Slowly, Abigail put on her best gown and stockings for the service. Had she been permitted a glass, she would have committed the sin of gazing into it today to assure herself that she did not look pale. She meant to arrive amidst the stares of the townsfolk with her head held high and a ruddy glow.

She left her room and made her way painfully down the steep stairs to the kitchen. Her younger sister, Franny, was sitting on the floor, playing with her cornhusk doll.

"Dorothy watered the garden for you today," Franny piped up. "But only because Mama said she must."

Abigail was relieved not to have to draw water from the well or tend to the garden this morning, but she knew that now she'd hear Dorothy complain of the extra work. Each of them had enough chores without adding more to their load.

Sarah Phelps, their maid, came into the room. She went to the fire and began to dish out food and place it on the table. While some townsfolk had been critical of the Faulkners for employing a maid, saying it smacked of excessiveness and an open display of wealth, Abigail knew that Sarah's family desperately needed the money. Because of this, Mama had kept her on, in spite of all the criticism.

Abigail held onto the back of Papa's chair to steady herself. "Good morrow," she said to Sarah.

"Your mother will be down straightaway, Abigail," Sarah said without looking at Abby.

Abigail's heart thudded at Sarah's curt response. They had always been friends, and Abigail was surprised that one transgression could change their friendship. It hurt her to see Sarah acting so cold.

And yet she had to face the truth. Sarah's reaction would be like many others today at Sabbath service. Abigail must prepare herself to handle the unforgiving looks of some and the averted eyes of others.

"Thank you, Sarah," Abigail said in her most civil voice. She began to help spread the food around the table. Though her muscles cried out in agony, Abigail mustered her courage and ignored the pain.

"Are you through with your chamber pot?" Sarah asked, still avoiding Abigail's eyes.

"Yes," Abigail said curtly. If this was the way Sarah was to act, so be it.

Mama came down the stairs. "Thank you, Sarah," she said. "I can manage now. I daresay you are most anxious to dress for the Sabbath service."

Sarah did a quick curtsy and left the room without a backward glance.

Mama touched the top of Abigail's head. "How are you today, Bear?"

"Weary," Abigail said, as her legs shook beneath her. She gripped the back of the chair more tightly.

"It's to be expected," Mama said. "I'll wager you'll feel like this for a day or so."

Mama went and took Franny's doll from her. "No playing on the Sabbath, little one, and breakfast is served."

Papa came into the kitchen, carrying Abigail's baby brother, Edward, in his arms. He said not a word to Abby, but handed Edward to Mama and sat to eat his breakfast. For once, Abigail welcomed his quiet ways. Other fathers might have added their own additional punishment to time in the stocks.

Dorothy came in from outside, clearly unhappy about her extra duties that morning.

"I am most grateful to you, Dorothy, for watering the garden today," Abigail said quietly.

Dorothy looked at Abigail for a moment. "The grubs have returned and are in the garden," she said grudgingly. "You'll need to use dried blood on the morrow."

Abigail nodded. Before she could say another word, her eight-year-old brother, Paul, came skidding into the house.

"You are tardy, Paul," Mama said. "Let me see your hands."

He held them out. They were black with dirt, a condition Paul tended to favor and Mama tended to bemoan.

"To the washbasin," Papa commanded.

Paul gave his hands a halfhearted scrub. When he was finished, his hands remained grimy.

"Paul, did you not see the dirt you were gathering on your hands this morning?" Mama said, smiling slightly as she took him back to the washbasin and began to scrub his hands with the rough lye soap. "Whatever were you doing?"

"I trapped that badger that has been plaguing the fields," Paul said. "He is a most goodly size."

"There is to be no trapping on the Sabbath, Paul," Papa said.

Paul ignored him. "Can I take him with us to meeting to show Steven?" he begged Mama.

The mention of her cousin brought a flush to Abigail's face. He was the one who had goaded her into racing yesterday. But *he* had not been caught, for he'd never finished the race, leaving her alone to face Elder Stevens at the end of the field, her skirts still high, her legs still pumping.

"I think a badger at Sabbath service would be unseemly, Paul," Mama said. "Now, let's eat. I am anxious to leave early today, as Abigail will be slower than usual."

Paul stood beside his siblings, while Mama and Papa sat at the plain board table. Papa gave thanks to the Lord, and they all began to eat. The room was quiet. They were not to talk during meals, and though Mama sometimes overlooked the rule, breaking it was never allowed on the Sabbath. The quiet was meant to prepare their souls for God.

When they finished, Mama rose. "Get your cloaks and caps, girls. Francis, can you get Edward?"

Papa did not respond, but instead began muttering to himself. Abigail recognized the tension in the air.

"Francis!" Mama spoke sharply. "It is time for the Sabbath service. Will you not walk with us to the meetinghouse?"

"Can't," Papa mumbled. "Why must they bother me so?" He began to rub his head, running his fingers over and over through his hair.

"Dorothy," Mama said, "get me a basin of warm water and some cloths. Quickly!"

Mama knelt in front of Papa. "Francis?" she said softly. "Francis? Can you hear me, dearest?"

Papa stared at her blankly.

She reached up and began to rub his temples. "Francis, can you hear me? Come, Francis. Let us go to the service."

Papa moaned and rocked his head back and forth. "Oh, why are you here for me again? Leave me alone! Leave me alone!"

Franny came and stood close to Abigail. She reached out and grabbed onto Abigail's gown. "Is Papa sick again?" she whispered.

Numbly, Abigail nodded. She hated when her father took with the fits. She hated the mutterings, the sullen moods, the unreasonable belief that someone was after him, and the violence, sometimes directed at others but mainly at himself. The doctors had examined him many times, but they could not understand what caused his fits. Some said he was taken with madness. But to Abigail it seemed as if he just became very confused and scared.

"Abigail, Paul, Franny"—Mama's voice was sharp—"get your cloaks and caps. Go on to service."

Abigail stared at her mother in shock. Go to service without Mama? Make the slow, painful walk to the meetinghouse by herself? Sit amidst all those staring eyes without Mama?

"Abigail," Mama said, "I'll have no argument on this. You'll go to Sabbath service without me!"

Dorothy brought over a large bowl of warm water and a clean linen cloth. Abigail grabbed Franny's hand and took her cloak from the peg by the door.

"Abigail?" Mama spoke, softer now.

Abigail turned to face her.

"Don't worry, Bear. Be brave and remember well who you are. I will be with you here"—Mama touched her own chest—"even if I am unable to be by your side."

Abigail bit her lip and took a deep breath. Mama was right. She could do this. Dorothy picked up Edward, and Abigail led Franny and Paul from the house. Behind her, Papa began to shout and cry.

"Abby?" Franny asked, as Abigail helped her into her cloak outside. "Will Papa be all right this time?"

Abigail wasn't sure, but she would not let Franny know that. Mama would want her to be strong, strong for Franny and Paul, and strong in front of the congregation.

"I'm sure he'll be fine, Franny," Abigail said. "Let me tie on your cap for you. We mustn't tarry now. Paul, button your coat."

Dorothy came outside and stood behind them. "It is an ill omen that this is happening today," she muttered. She had Edward's coat and began to put it on him, roughly forcing his arms into the sleeves, causing him to cry out in protest.

"Be gentle with him," Abigail said.

Dorothy gave Abigail an embarrassed look, then hugged little Edward to her. "I'm sorry, Edward," she whispered to him. Abigail could see the worry in her sister's face.

Together, the Faulkner children began the short walk to town. The outside air was chilly for a late May morning, and Abigail pulled her red cloak close about her.

Franny held Abigail's hand, but their progress was slow. Abigail's hips and legs hurt with each step she took. Paul and Dorothy walked quickly on ahead with Edward.

As they neared town, the meetinghouse bells rang out. Abigail's pulse quickened. She lifted her head and went forward to face the upcoming sermon, mustering all her courage and wishing that Mama were there.

three

As the family neared the meetinghouse, they heard parishioners calling greetings to one another. Children were gathered in little groups, happy that on the Sabbath they had fewer chores and more time to see other children from the village, even if there was no running or playing allowed. Abby saw her cousin, Steven, off with one group. He saw her, too, and he grinned and stuck out his tongue at her. Abigail did the same.

But as she grew closer to the meetinghouse, the noise died off, and silence enveloped Abigail and her brothers and sisters.

"It seems we're all to suffer today because of your sin," Dorothy said, tears in her eyes.

Abigail was hurt by Dorothy's harsh words, but she knew her sister. Dorothy worried all the time, and often when she was concerned about something, she was unaware of how harshly she spoke. Abigail forgave Dorothy her comments, for she knew Dorothy loved her in spite of her transgression. The townspeople, who were now giving her the silent treatment, Abigail could less easily forgive.

"What ho," whispered a voice in Abigail's ear.

Abigail turned to find her mother's sister behind her. Aunt Elizabeth reached out and tightly grasped Abigail's arm. Her husband, Daniel, swept Franny up into his arms.

"Uncle Daniel! Uncle Daniel! Put me down!" Franny shrieked.

Daniel set Franny down, smiling at her. Then he leaned in toward Abigail.

"What, niece, no smile on the Sabbath?" Uncle Daniel said. "Pray, Abby, pay them all little attention."

Abigail felt relief run through her. Aunt Elizabeth and Uncle Daniel were considered among the most beloved and devout of the town. No one would dare ignore them.

"Greetings, Goody Sprague," Aunt Elizabeth

called out, as they approached the meetinghouse, her grip tight on Abigail's arm.

"Good day, Mistress Johnson," Goodwife Sprague replied.

Though her reply to Aunt Elizabeth was courteous, Abigail could feel the woman's eyes upon her, unforgiving and critical.

"Good day, Goody Sprague," Abigail said, lifting her head defiantly to look at the woman.

Goody Sprague glared at Abigail. Turning toward Aunt Elizabeth, she said, "A man with a firm hand would stop that one from her sinful ways." Then, sweeping up her skirts, Goodwife Sprague left them to enter the meetinghouse.

Abigail could feel her cheeks redden, but she kept her head high.

Uncle Daniel grinned at her side. "That one wishes she could *find* a man with a firm hand."

"Daniel!" Aunt Elizabeth protested, blushing, but Abigail saw her smile slightly.

Then her aunt turned toward her. "Pray tell, Abby, where are your mother and father that you are to face this criticism alone?"

"Papa is ill," Franny piped up. "He couldn't come with us. Someone's after him."

Aunt Elizabeth's eyes widened. "But he has been so much better of late," she protested. "Are you certain?"

Dorothy shivered. "'Tis probably the Lord's way of punishing us for Abigail's indecent act."

"Nonsense, Dorothy," Aunt Elizabeth replied. "Your father's fits have naught to do with Abigail."

The bells of the meetinghouse tolled again.

"Come," Uncle Daniel said. "Today of all days, we shouldn't tarry, or we will bring the wrath of Goody Sprague and the others down upon us all."

Aunt Elizabeth nodded. "Here," she said to Dorothy, "I'll carry Edward. Where is that rascal Paul?"

"He ran on ahead with Steven," Dorothy said.

Aunt Elizabeth looked at her husband. "Daniel, go on ahead. Be sure Paul and Steven are behaving themselves. Abigail, have you Franny?"

Abigail nodded, but her throat tightened as they neared the doors.

"Now, remember," Aunt Elizabeth said, "do not

pay attention to the looks, Abigail. Be brave and bear it well, just as you did with Goody Sprague."

Together they entered the meetinghouse, and Abigail prepared herself for what would perhaps feel like the longest day of her life. The sermon would be for her. It would be about her. It would be long and fiery, and though Abigail might question the validity of God's command not to lift her skirts and race for pleasure, on the subject of the sermon she had no doubts.

The first two hours of service were always difficult, as Abby knew two more hours were to come after the midday meal. But today was harder. Abigail's legs ached and the rough cloth of her gown chafed against her skin. Though the late spring day had grown warm, the meetinghouse was still cold from the long winter. The hard wooden seats were unforgiving, and Abby could not find a position that didn't cause her pain.

During the midday meal, Abigail and the others stayed in town to eat. Abigail had hoped Mama and Papa would join them, but they did not come, and she began to worry about them as she slowly ate her bread and sausage.

Paul, Franny, and Dorothy went off to eat with the other children, but Abigail stayed with Aunt Elizabeth, Uncle Daniel, and Edward. She did not want to listen to any possible taunts and teasing.

After the break, when Grandpappy came to the pulpit, his eyes turned toward Abigail. He looked troubled, and she felt awful that today he would be forced to lecture her publicly. She stiffened, yet did not move her gaze from his. She heard the satisfied sounds of the townspeople behind her. They seemed almost gleeful to have their minister tongue-lash his own granddaughter.

But when Grandpappy's readings from the Bible came, they were not what Abigail, nor anyone else, had expected. He did not choose God's passages on sinful behavior. He did not speak about indecency.

Abigail was relieved, though puzzled, and then troubled. Would Grandpappy not speak about her? Would he refuse to mention her sin and thereby open himself up for criticism? As much as she disliked being the center of the town's ridicule, much less would she like it if her Grandfather suffered for not addressing her publicly as he did all others who had faced time in the stocks.

Beside her, Aunt Elizabeth sat with her eyebrows raised. Abigail could stand it no longer. Though she knew it was wrong to speak in the meetinghouse, she had to ask.

"Why does he not speak of my sin?" she whispered to her aunt.

Aunt Elizabeth gave her a stern look, but Abigail could see that she was confused also.

"Let no man lie nor make false accusations in the face of the Lord!" Grandpappy's voice bellowed out. "So sayeth the Lord."

"What does this have to do with anything?" Dorothy asked, her voice shaking.

Aunt Elizabeth made a motion with her hand for Dorothy to be quiet. She looked around, but the tithing man had not heard their whispering. If he had, they would have been tapped on the shoulder and their family fined for speaking during services. The tithing man had a sharp eye and a heavy rod, and it was lucky they had escaped his notice.

"It is one of our dear Lord's commandments, and it must be obeyed!" yelled out Reverend Dane. "Thou shalt not bear false witness against thy neighbor!"

Her grandfather's voice was loud and angry.

What was he talking about? If his lecture had directly concerned her behavior, she would have been warm with the shame. But lying? This sermon was not for her.

Abigail stole a quick glance behind her. The rest of the congregation looked as puzzled as she felt. They were looking at one another, their eyes clouded with confusion.

"Break one of these commandments," shouted Grandpappy, "and thou art doomed to damnation for eternity!"

Abigail shivered at the word damnation. She hated it. *If salvation was so hard to get,* Abby wondered, *why did everyone keep on hoping for it?* Abigail had long ago resigned herself to hell. Try as she might, she had sinned a lot and often, both in thoughts and in deeds. She knew there was little hope for her redemption. The gaping jaws of hell loomed large for her, but only when she thought of it, which was on Sunday. The rest of the week, death and its ultimate penalty seemed a long way off.

"Let us pray," Reverend Dane whispered.

The sudden softness of his voice startled Abigail, and she dropped her head. She listened to her grandfather pray for their souls. The four-hour service had almost ended, and still no word for her. Something was wrong.

"Amen," her grandfather said, and he turned and left the pulpit.

There was silence in the meetinghouse. Everyone was stunned. Then, behind her, Abigail heard the low mumbling of dissatisfaction. Grandpappy would pay dearly for not having talked about her today. There was a lump in Abigail's throat.

"Come," Aunt Elizabeth whispered, "let us take our leave. There is much anger here, and I think it best if we depart immediately."

"Why did he do it?" Dorothy asked. "Why did he not address the question of seemly behavior?"

"Why is everyone acting so strangely, Aunt Lizzy?" Franny asked.

"Not now, Franny," Aunt Elizabeth said. "Come. Let us go see to your mother."

"But shouldn't we stay to be with Grandpappy?" Abigail asked, forgetting her own fear of facing the congregation.

Aunt Elizabeth sighed. "Truly, I wish I knew which choice would be best. Your mother needs us now with your father, but surely your Grandpappy will need us to help him set things right with the townspeople. And yet it would not be seemly to divide as a family, either."

"Then let me suggest that we go to the aid of your sister first," Uncle Daniel said, having come with Edward and Paul from the men's side of the meetinghouse. "Your father is an intelligent man, Elizabeth, and he chose to do what he did today for some purpose. I am certain he is aware of what he will have to endure, with or without your support."

Aunt Elizabeth nodded. "Aye, husband. You speak wisely. Let us hurry to my sister's and find out what awaits us there."

Aunt Elizabeth gathered Edward up and took Franny by the hand. Abigail followed Uncle Daniel, Paul, and Dorothy, but she paused on the meeting-house steps.

Outside, the townspeople gathered, surly looks upon their faces. They turned their disapproving, angry glances upon Abigail. The elders stared at her.

Aunt Elizabeth, however, continued on, sweeping up her skirts and marching past the congregation. Uncle Daniel came and took Abigail's and Dorothy's arms, and together they hurried after Aunt Elizabeth.

Abigail could feel the eyes of the congregation following them up the hill toward home. In spite of everything, she almost wished to turn back and face them. What lay ahead, she knew, would probably be worse.

four

There was an eerie silence in the house. Abigail and her family stood just inside the doorway, not moving. Everything was in place. The fireplace was freshly swept and sanded, a few embers still burning. The pewter gleamed and shone with polish. Fresh herbs hung from the rafters to dry. The spinning wheel stood ready for use. The loom held cloth for a new dress for Franny. Still, an odd tension seemed to fill the air.

Aunt Elizabeth turned, startling them all. "Abigail," she commanded, "go at once and fetch some firewood to get the fire going again. Dorothy, check if your mother and father are upstairs."

Aunt Elizabeth strode into the kitchen, Edward on her hip.

Abigail felt a lump in her throat. What would Dorothy find upstairs? Had Papa finally done himself damage in trying to elude the figures he always felt were chasing him? Had he hurt Mama in the process? She remembered all the times the doctors had tried to figure out what was wrong with Papa. They had bled him, changed his diet, and prayed over him. Finally they had shrugged their shoulders and told Mama that there was nothing they could do to remove these strange, dark fits he had.

"Please don't tarry, Abigail," Aunt Elizabeth admonished, setting Edward on the floor. "The fire is almost out, and there's the Sabbath meal to warm."

"What shall I do, Aunt Lizzy?" Franny piped up.

"Here, Franny," Aunt Elizabeth said, removing Edward's jacket, "watch over your little brother for me and keep him quiet."

Paul was sidling toward the door, but Aunt Elizabeth saw him out of the corner of her eye. "And you, young man, go out with Abigail and bring in some kindling."

"Bringing in kindling is tomorrow's chore," Paul complained.

"Stop your griping, Paul, and go," Aunt Elizabeth said, removing her cloak and cap. "You too, Abigail. Quickly now. We have much to do."

But Abigail could not leave until Dorothy came down the steep front stairs. She descended slowly, carrying a pewter mug.

"Some linens were shredded," Dorothy said softly, "and a chair was upended. The rooms are empty."

Aunt Elizabeth's face went white. Mama and Papa were not in the house, and it was growing dark outside.

"Are Mama and Papa all right?" Franny asked.

"They're probably out having some sport, leaving us with their chores," Paul muttered.

Aunt Elizabeth shot him an angry glance. Then she turned to Uncle Daniel. He nodded, and without Aunt Elizabeth saying a word, picked up his hat. "I'll return with news as quickly as I can," he said.

Abigail followed him out into the cool evening air, shutting the door behind her. She walked after him, down the path between the vegetable and herb gardens to the wooden gate in front of their house. "Uncle Daniel?" she called softly.

He turned. "Aye, Abigail?"

"It will be all right, won't it?" she asked.

Visions of Papa doing himself some terrible harm and accidentally injuring Mama filled Abigail's head.

Uncle Daniel had no words of comfort for her. "I cannot say, Abigail. Your father is terrible to see when the fits take him. We can only pray your mother and her reason will protect him this time as before."

He turned, and Abigail watched him walk away into the evening's darkness, down the rutted road toward the village. She tried to hold onto some small hope that Papa was well, but the emptiness of the house seemed to indicate differently.

Quickly, Abigail gathered up a load of firewood. Her sore legs caused her to shake a little as she lifted the heavy load.

Paul came out of the house. He picked up a rock and sent it flying into the road. "I'll have to see to the cows myself tonight," he complained. "When I'm older, I'm going to have fits every day so *I* can avoid all manner of chores."

"Paul," Abigail admonished, "you are tempting the devil with words such as those. You do not want Papa's fits."

"I do if it means I don't have to tend to the cows," Paul muttered.

Abigail could not help herself. Even with the situation as it was, and knowing it was a sin on the Sabbath, she had to laugh. Paul always looked at things from his perspective. There was no other.

"Abigail," Dorothy called from the house, "Paul. Hurry with the wood!"

Paul rolled his eyes, but he came and lifted some of the wood from Abigail's arms. "You must still be weary after yesterday," he said gruffly.

Abigail started to thank him, but Paul sighed and said, "If you had kept your senses, you wouldn't be sore at all."

He glanced sternly back at her, but Abigail could see his eyes were soft. Though her little brother was often troublesome, there was always this other side to him. Abigail loved him for it.

They carried the load into the house, where Aunt Elizabeth and Dorothy were laying out the evening meal, gathering together the pewter mugs and wooden plates and spoons. Paul soon had the fire going again.

On the wooden floor, Edward was up on all

fours, wiggling as he tried unsuccessfully to move himself forward. Franny had taken Aunt Elizabeth at her word and wasn't letting Edward crawl around. This was frustrating Edward to no end, as he loved movement and lots of it. He let out a wail, and Franny picked him up and cuddled him to her. Edward fought to be put back down, and Franny fought equally hard to contain him. The scene was almost comical. Everything *inside* seemed normal.

"Abigail," said Aunt Elizabeth, "concentrate on the Sabbath meal and turn away from unpleasant thoughts. Your worrying will come to naught anyway."

Abigail nodded and joined her sister at the fire to help with the meal. Soon the leftover bean porridge was warming in the pot over the fire. Its heady smell filled the room, and a rosy glow from the fire encircled them all.

The warmth of the scene was brought to a halt by a loud banging on the door. Aunt Elizabeth nodded to Dorothy, who hurried to open the door. Abigail prayed the caller was not someone with bad news.

But the person standing out in the misty evening was Grandpappy. He entered, shaking droplets from his cloak and hat. Tiny beads of moisture had gathered in his bushy brows.

"Pray tell, where were the likes of you following the service?" he asked everyone.

His eyes fell on Abigail. "Especially you, young lady. You escaped your just punishment today, for which I will pay most dearly, and you should have had the graciousness to be beside me when the elders came to criticize me."

Grandpappy suddenly stopped. An understanding came into his eyes as he realized that Mama and Papa were not there.

"Where's Francis?" he asked, his voice low and worried.

Aunt Elizabeth bit her lower lip.

"Off having a fit," Paul said, scowling.

"Ah, no," Grandpappy said. He walked over and sank onto a stool by the fire. "This cannot be happening again, not now."

He glanced at Aunt Elizabeth. "Tell me quickly, child. What brought it on this time?"

Aunt Elizabeth shrugged. "I know not, Father. It happened early at breakfast when I was at my own home with Daniel."

Grandpappy's eyes lit on Abigail. "Were you here?"

Abigail nodded. "I was, but I had slept late. At breakfast, Papa was already ill."

Grandpappy's eyebrows drew together. "Slept late? On the Sabbath? My daughter spoils you, Abigail."

He then turned to Paul. "Were you witness to your father's decline this morning?"

"No," Paul said quickly.

"He was out chasing a badger," Franny interjected.

"On the Sabbath?" Grandpappy said, his eyes darkening.

"He's been in the fields, tearing everything up," Paul defended himself. "I had a chance to finally get him. I couldn't just let him go."

Grandpappy looked skeptically at Paul, who blushed.

"I was here, Grandpappy," Dorothy spoke up. "Papa's sickness came about when Mama began to speak of Abigail and what she would face this morning, urging Papa to let her sleep. Papa agreed at first, but then he began to mumble that someone might punish him for letting her sleep. That was when he started his mutterings."

Abigail stopped stirring the porridge. She was no

longer hungry, now that she realized her actions might have brought about her father's fit.

Grandpappy sighed. "Where are they now?"

"Daniel has gone to search them out," Aunt Elizabeth responded.

"Bring me a drink, Elizabeth," Grandpappy bade her. "I will wait here with you for news. 'Tis not good that this illness is upon Francis again. It could come at no worse time."

"Grandpappy," Dorothy said, coming close to him, "what caused you to speak as you did today at the Sabbath service, and to avoid talking about Abigail?"

Grandpappy gazed into the fire. "If more important matters did not need to be talked about, your sister would have suffered the full force of my wrath. But there are greater issues that have come to my attention of late." He paused. "I fear your father's illness will be linked to these matters if we are not careful."

He looked up at the family, his eyes troubled. "Say naught of this fit to anyone. Let us hope that Francis has done nothing to draw attention to his illness this time, and that the night watch does not see them out and about. Let us pray that Daniel finds them safely and brings them back quietly."

Aunt Elizabeth brought him a warm mug of cider. "Of what are you so fearful, Father?"

Grandpappy shook his head. "News has come that the devil has been discovered in Salem Village. They are uncovering witches there at a furious pace."

Abigail drew in her breath. The devil in Salem Village? The small village was but a day's ride from Andover. Her earlier thoughts of hell and damnation closed upon her like a hand at her throat.

"But how does that affect us?" Paul scoffed. "There are no witches here in Andover."

"Nor perhaps in Salem Village," Grandpappy said, "but that may not stop the townspeople."

"What do you mean, Grandpappy?" Dorothy asked.

"Child, your father, with his illness, is an oddity." Grandpappy sighed deeply. "An oddity that may just bring about our ruin."

Abigail looked at her grandfather's serious face. The room, which a minute ago had been warm and cozy, suddenly seemed cold.

five

They had barely finished their Sabbath meal when Abigail heard a muffled noise. Paul had gone out to bring in the cows, but it was too early for him to be back. She glanced up and saw that Grandpappy and Aunt Elizabeth had heard it too. All eyes turned toward the door.

"Dorothy," Grandpappy said roughly, "let them in."

Dorothy rose swiftly and opened the door. No one was on the stoop, but the odd sounds continued in the darkness.

"Mama?" Dorothy called out softly.

"Aye, Dorothy, 'tis I," Mama called back. "We'll be there shortly."

Aunt Elizabeth went to the door. "Do you need help, Hannah?"

"Nay, sister," Mama said. "Daniel is with me."

A moment later, they were close enough to the house for Abigail to see them. Uncle Daniel was on one side of Papa, holding him up, and Mama was on the other. Papa was mumbling and seemed dazed and confused.

Relief flooded through Abigail when she saw that Mama was all right. But then she noticed that her mother had no cap or cloak and that her face was pale.

Grandpappy rose from the table. "I will take him," he said.

Grandpappy was a big man, and he walked outside into the light rain and lifted Papa as if he were a baby. He carried him inside and up the stairs. Abigail could hear his heavy footsteps going toward Mama and Papa's bedchamber, then the creak of the bed as Grandpappy lay Papa upon it. Uncle Daniel came in and sat down on a stool, taking off his hat and rubbing his eyes. On the floor beside him, Edward was asleep on a blanket.

Mama went toward the stairs to follow Grandpappy.

"Hannah, wait," Aunt Elizabeth said. "You look

exhausted. You must eat something. I'll wager you've had naught since breakfast."

Mama smiled weakly. "'Tis true. It has been a most difficult day. But I must see to Francis, Eliza."

"I will do that," Aunt Elizabeth said. "You are soaked to the bone, and you will be no good for Francis should you sicken. Come sit by the fire and warm yourself."

Mama looked up the stairs and then sighed. "I admit I am most weary, and my hunger is great."

Aunt Elizabeth climbed the stairs to help Grandpappy, and Abigail went quickly to the fire and dished out two bowls of bean porridge, one for Mama and one for Uncle Daniel. Mama sat down by the fire, next to Uncle Daniel, and Dorothy poured them both some hot cider. Franny brought bread from the table.

Abigail placed the bowl in her mother's hands. She could see that her mother was shaking, so she ran to the door and got her own dry, warm cloak to place on her mother's shoulders. "Here, Mama."

Mama smiled at her. "Thank you, Bear," she said.

Then her smile suddenly disappeared. "But I had almost forgotten. Pray tell me, Abigail, how fared you today at the Sabbath service?"

Abigail was about to reply, but before she could speak, Dorothy came and sat beside Mama.

"Abigail was given no tongue-lashing, Mama," Dorothy said. "Grandpappy's sermon was directed at Salem Village. Witches have been discovered there."

Mama's eyes widened, and again Abby felt a cold chill at the mention of witches and the thought of their devil's work.

"Lord," Mama breathed. "This is a most frightful thing to consider."

"Have you ever seen a witch, Mama?" Franny asked, leaning against her.

Mama shook her head. "I have not, child, and I pray I never do."

Grandpappy's footsteps sounded on the stairs.

"Is it true, Father?" Mama asked. "Is there devilry in Salem Village?"

Grandpappy shot Mama a quick glance. "Let us not speak of this matter in front of the children now. I do not believe they should hear the depth of what we must discuss. More importantly, daughter, tell me quickly: Were others aware of your husband's condition today?"

Mama glanced into the fire. "I fear so, Father. Francis did take with a most terrible fit. He believed he saw shapes in the widow Browning's leaded windows, and he broke four of them in his panic."

Grandpappy sighed. "Is it possible that no one saw Francis doing this damage? Dare I hope he did his destruction during my Sabbath sermon?"

Mama shook her head. "It was following the meeting, Father. In truth, Francis was breaking the windows just as the widow Browning was coming home from the meetinghouse."

Abigail glanced over at Dorothy, who looked troubled. Above them, Papa moaned, and Aunt Elizabeth spoke, soft and soothing.

"Mama," Franny said, "will they do something to Papa because he broke the windows?" She plucked at her mother's sleeve.

Daniel, who had been steadily eating his supper, spoke. "The townsfolk are quite aware of your father's condition, Franny, and of the fits that take him now and again. I'm sure the widow Browning will be most kind in accepting payment for the replacement of her windows."

He looked pointedly at Mama and Grandpappy.

Mama took the hint at once and rose from her stool by the fire. "Thank you, girls, for a most delicious meal, but I believe it is time to get these little ones abed. Dorothy, I will leave you to attend to the cleaning up. Abigail, come help me with Edward. Franny, run ahead and ready yourself for bed, child. Now where's Paul got off to?"

"He went to bring in the cows before you came home," Abigail replied.

Mama nodded. "Good boy," she said. "Come along then, Bear. I am most weary and would welcome your help tonight."

Abigail picked up Edward and followed Mama and Franny up the stairs. But from the corner of her eye, she saw Grandpappy and Uncle Daniel pulling their stools closer to the fire, and bending their heads, one to the other. And she wished with all her might that she could hear their talk tonight.

Mama tucked Dorothy, Abigail, and Franny into their beds, laying a hand tenderly upon each of their cheeks before going back down the stairs.

Abigail lay in the dark, looking up at the ceiling

and thinking about all that Grandpappy had said that night.

"Dorothy," she whispered, "do you think that sometimes Papa has the devil with him? Could it be possible that one day we shall be like him too?"

Dorothy turned her white-capped head toward Abby. "Hush," she whispered. "We mustn't frighten Franny."

"I'm not frightened," Franny spoke up from where she lay in the bed across the room. "I know Papa's no devil."

Abigail smiled in the darkness. She remembered how easy it was to be brave at the age of six.

"Go to sleep, Franny," Dorothy said. "You are sensible not to worry. Grandpappy will see to Papa and Mama. He always does."

Then Dorothy turned toward Abby. "You go to sleep too, sister. There is naught we can do tonight. You and Franny and I are not weak in the head like Papa. He has been this way a long time, and I'll wager Grandpappy will have the sympathy of the town on our side before the morrow."

"Aye, Dorothy," Abigail replied, turning as if she

intended to sleep. But she did not, and when at last she felt her elder sister's body slacken beside her and heard Franny's soft and steady breath from across the room, she rose from the bed and tiptoed out of the room. Silently, she tread down the steep stairs until she could see Uncle Daniel, Mama, Grandpappy, and Aunt Elizabeth and hear all they had to say.

"You are certain then, sir?" Uncle Daniel asked.

Grandpappy nodded. "As certain as one can be in these matters. I sat with the other ministers and watched these young girls. Their fits are most frightful to see. They twist and moan and clutch at their arms as if being made to perform in ways most unwanted by them."

Abigail drew in her breath. Young *girls* were being tormented by the devil?

"If it is so fearful then," Aunt Elizabeth said, "what makes you certain that it is not in fact the devil that takes them?"

Grandpappy shook his head. "I do not believe in witchcraft, Elizabeth. I think the girls are doing nothing more than having a bit of sport."

"Sport that is causing chaos," Uncle Daniel said

angrily. "If the girls are truly lying, they should be punished."

Were the girls lying? Abigail wondered. It seemed an awful and ugly thing to do. But if the devil was not in Salem Village, and the girls were only playing a game, Abigail knew quite well the punishment they would receive. She touched her own legs as a reminder. Racing for pleasure was a small offense. Lying was a much greater one.

Or was it the devil himself who was making them lie? On the stairs, Abigail shuddered. She knew herself to be brave, but how did one go about fighting off the devil?

"Father," Mama said, "if the girls are lying, why does no one stop them?"

Grandpappy sighed. "It is as if the town has gone mad out there. I am at a loss to explain it, daughter. But the people of Salem Village believe the girls."

"Can no one put an end to this madness, then?" Mama asked.

"Nay," Grandpappy said. "It seems not. Already they have convicted three people of witchcraft: a slave woman named Tituba, an old beggar woman named Sarah Good, and an ungodly woman, Sarah

Osborne. All of them are oddities, daughter. Do you understand my concern now?"

"But surely this will not come to Andover, sir," Uncle Daniel said. "We are a God-fearing, sensible lot here."

"I hope you are right, Daniel, but I fear it may," Grandpappy said. "I kept my own thoughts at the meeting of ministers this time, but it could become necessary that I speak out against the girls should this madness spread."

A log fell into the fire, throwing up sparks.

"If it does," Grandpappy continued, "Francis's condition could be thought to have the work of the devil about it."

The door opened, and Paul came inside. He stared at the four of them, huddled around the fire.

"The cows are in," he said roughly.

"I am most grateful, Paul," Mama said. "Your father will be also when he is himself again."

Paul gave a short bark of a laugh.

"Mind your tongue," Grandpappy said sharply, "or you'll be seeing the strap of my belt. Off to bed with you."

Paul made his way toward the stairs.

Abigail stood, suddenly aware that she was to be discovered. She turned to flee, but not before Mama looked up and saw her. Their eyes met, and Abigail saw that Mama, too, was frightened.

six

Papa woke Abigail and Dorothy

at first light the next morning. Abigail looked into his eyes and saw that they were clear. His fit had passed. Yet his face showed signs of worry.

"Your mother is with fever," Papa said, his voice low and urgent. "I have sat with her for a goodly portion of this early morning, but I fear she worsens."

Papa's face flushed. Abigail knew he realized that it was his fault their mother was sick. She tried to feel some sympathy, but instead felt only frustration with him. Mama was ill, and being out with Papa in the wet night had probably brought that sickness on.

"Dorothy," Papa said, "begin preparing this morning's breakfast. Sarah should be here soon to help you. Let Franny sleep until Edward wakens and then have her watch over him. Abigail, I would have you be with your mother while I am away. I must tend to the livestock, but I won't be gone long."

"Aye, Papa," Dorothy said. "I'll be down shortly. Leave us to dress."

Papa nodded. "Thank you," he said, his voice thick with emotion. Then he turned and left.

Abigail climbed from the bed. Quietly, so as not to wake Franny, she slipped on her homespun dress and tied an apron over it. Dorothy, too, dressed hurriedly. She bundled her long hair into her cap and strode from the room.

Abigail finished washing her face and then walked toward her parents' bedroom. Inside, she could hear the low murmur of voices. She went to the door.

Papa was sitting on the edge of the bed, his head bowed. Mama, flushed with fever, was holding his hand.

"Now, Francis," she said softly, "please do not blame yourself for my condition. It might have been that I would have sickened anyway. I had not felt right the last few days."

Papa drew Mama's hand to his lips. Abigail saw him press a kiss into her palm.

"I am not worthy of you, Hannah," he whispered.

"Hush, Francis," Mama said. "Do not say such things."

Then she looked up and saw Abby standing in the doorway.

"Go, Francis," she said. "Abigail is here. Go on out and take Paul. I will be well watched over, and I shall be myself again before the morrow."

Papa rose, his eyes not leaving Mama's. He bent and quickly kissed her on the forehead. He walked toward Abigail. "Will you call me, Abby, should she worsen?" he asked.

Abigail nodded, even as she felt her anger rise. If Mama worsened, *he* was the cause! But could he have helped it? Abby had to stop these angry feelings. She knew they were wrong. He was her father, and she should respect him.

Papa patted Abby's head and left the room.

Mama smiled weakly at her. "Come, Abby," she said. "Sit by me. There is much weaving and spinning we must attend to today, and Dorothy has to be sure to put bread in early this morning."

"Mama, please do not concern yourself with

household duties," Abigail said, pulling up a chair beside her mother. "Dorothy and I can handle things."

Mama smiled again. "I know you can, Bear."

Her eyes closed. "And being quite aware of that fact, I will rest awhile. I am weary, Bear, very weary."

Mama was soon sleeping, but the sleep was not restful. She tossed and turned, moaning slightly. Sarah brought breakfast, leaving it on the bedside table. She did not say a word to Abigail, but Abby was too preoccupied with her mother to be concerned about that today.

Dorothy came upstairs midmorning. She pushed aside the bed curtains and reached over to touch Mama's forehead. Her face fell.

"She is burning with fever," Dorothy said. "Would that I could go and fetch Doctor Cushman. But Franny and Edward need looking after, the fire and the bread need tending, and Mama needs you beside her."

"Why can't you send Sarah for the doctor?" Abigail asked.

"Sarah is leaving us. She has made it plain that she doesn't wish to be in a household where the master is taken with fits and the children with indecent acts."

Abigail stared at Dorothy. "Can Sarah truly believe this is an evil household?" she asked. "Mama has been so kind to her. We all have."

"Aye," Dorothy said scornfully, "but I believe she tends to forget our kindnesses."

Mama sat up suddenly, her eyes unfocused.

"Mama?" Dorothy asked.

But Mama said nothing. She did not seem to notice Abigail and Dorothy in the room. She pulled the bedsheets up about her, shivering, and her eyes grew wide and frightened.

"Nay!" Mama screamed out. "Nay, I will not come!"

Abigail jumped at the suddenness of the outburst. She and Dorothy stared in horror at Mama, whose eyes were rolling about. Her head swayed back and forth.

"It must be the fever," Abby whispered, trying to convince herself.

"Run, quickly," Dorothy whispered back. "Run for Papa, Abigail. Tell him Mama worsens."

Abigail gathered up her skirts. She ran toward the door and into the hallway, where she saw Sarah. From the way she stared at her, Abigail knew she had heard Mama. Sarah turned and fled down the stairs with Abigail close on her heels.

"Sarah!" Abby called.

But Sarah did not turn around.

"Watch after Edward," Abigail yelled to Franny. "I'm going for Papa."

She ran after Sarah, out into the warm May air. Sarah looked back at Abigail, her eyes wide with fright. Abby wished she could follow her, calm her fears, and talk her into staying, for they needed her now more than ever, but she knew she must fetch Papa first. So Abigail turned and ran, her skirts up, toward Papa's fields at the edge of town. This time, there was no pleasure in the running.

seven

Later that day, Abigail sat doing her mending by the fire. Yet she couldn't concentrate, and she pricked her finger with the needle several times. Crying out in frustration, she finally gave up and threw the mending into the basket. How she hated sewing!

Franny came and put her head in Abby's lap. "Will Mama be all right?" Franny asked.

Abigail did not answer. She didn't know what to say.

Dorothy picked up Edward, who began to cry. He squirmed around in her arms, trying desperately to escape.

"Hush," Dorothy scolded. Yet Abigail saw her draw Edward near and kiss his head.

Finally, there were footsteps on the stairs. Abigail rose from her place by the fire as Papa and Doctor Cushman descended.

"I cannot tell you, Francis," the doctor said. "Only the Lord knows for sure if she will come out of this. I fear the child may be having a bad time of it too."

Child? Abigail thought. *What child?* And then she knew. Mama was pregnant again. It was probably why she had not been feeling right these past few days. Abby was concerned now not just for Mama but for her new brother or sister, as well. She knew that sometimes if a mother was taken with fever while pregnant, the child would not be right when born.

The doctor went to the door and picked up his hat and cloak. "I will keep you in my prayers, Francis," he said, "but there is naught that I can do for her now." Then he left.

Papa turned to his children. His face was drawn, his forehead creased with worry.

"She will be better," he whispered softly, as if to convince himself that it was true.

No one said a word. Even Franny seemed to know that she shouldn't ask questions now.

"Come, Papa," Dorothy said quietly. "Supper is ready. Abigail, go and call for Paul. Franny, wash your hands."

Abigail watched Dorothy carry Edward toward the table. Normally, she would have been angry at Dorothy for giving them all orders, but today she was glad for it. In commanding them all to keep busy, Dorothy had given them something to think about other than Mama.

The weeks passed slowly. Abigail and Dorothy did the chores around the house, cooking and cleaning and washing and mending. Because Aunt Elizabeth had no children of her own to tend to, she was able to find time between her own household chores to come by and lend a hand as well. Yet every night, Abigail fell wearily into bed beside Dorothy, sleeping heavily until light poured in the leaded windows the next day. Never had she been so aware of the many difficult chores Sarah had handled.

Grandpappy came daily for dinner, his eyes worried, his prayers at the supper table long. Papa went about his work quietly, but Abigail often saw him outside, his eyes turned toward their bedroom window. He brought Mama flowers daily, filling their bedroom with all her favorite kinds. One day he even rode all the way to Salem Town to bring Mama unusual teas and a fancy plate from England, items that must have cost him much.

Abigail realized he was torn up inside, and yet she could not forgive him his fits. She knew he could not stop them from coming, and he was paying the price for them now. But still she wished he could try to be stronger and battle the dark thoughts that consumed him at times.

At last, Mama began to recover, but her progress was slow. Abigail thanked the Lord every morning and every evening as she saw Mama's strength returning, and she made a promise to the Lord never to race again. It seemed a small price to pay for Mama's restored health.

eight

Summer came to Andover.

Mud gave way to green fields, and farmers were busy from sunup to sundown. Edward began to walk, delighting everyone with his joy at what he could now do.

Mama continued to recover slowly, rising late and walking a little more each day. Papa walked with her in the evenings. They would stroll to the top of the hill and watch the sunset, Mama leaning on Papa's arm. Abigail was grateful for Papa's caring. During these weeks, Mama's belly began to grow bigger, and Abigail wondered if the child would recover from the fever too, or if damage had been done by the illness.

One day, Mama stopped her flax spinning and stood, stretching slightly.

"Abby," she said. "Gather up Edward and come with me. I feel the need for a turn out of doors."

"Shall I call Dorothy and Franny, too?" Abigail asked.

Mama shook her head. "They are busy gathering berries. I can manage with just you."

Abigail was delighted. It was a rare time these days when she was alone with Mama, or at least alone with Mama and Edward. They put on their cloaks and opened the door. Sunshine poured in and warmed Abigail's face.

"'Tis a beautiful day," Mama said. "Let us walk a bit."

Abigail lifted Edward onto her hip and put a steadying hand on Mama's arm.

"Thank you, Bear," Mama said.

Slowly they began walking up the hill, away from the village. When they reached the top, the world seemed to lie at their feet. The meadows in front of them shone in the sunshine, and Abigail listened with a joyful heart to the sounds of the birds. She felt a deep longing to lift her skirts and run, but then, she remembered her promise.

Mama breathed deeply. "'Tis a lovely smell, that

smell of earth," she said. "Come, Abby. Let us spread our cloaks upon the ground and sit for a bit. I believe we can spare a minute in this sunshine if we don't tarry too long."

Abby quickly loosened her cloak and spread it on the ground. Mama lowered herself slowly, and Abigail placed Edward beside her. Edward did not stay still long. He stood on his wobbly legs and was soon off exploring the tall grasses in front of them, falling often on his behind, making Mama and Abby laugh.

Abigail sat down and laid her head in Mama's lap. Mama stroked her hair, singing softly. Abigail closed her eyes, letting the sunshine soak into her body. It was peaceful, but she longed to jump up and take off, like a bird all on its own, winging her way through the summer air.

"You are as restless as a sheep about to be shorn, Bear," Mama said, chuckling. "The meadow is a fine place for a bit of sport. Go on, run. Lift your skirts. There is no one to see you but me."

"Nay, Mama," Abigail said. "When your fever broke, I made a promise to the Lord never to race like that again."

Mama laughed. "'Twas a noble idea you had, Abby. But I daresay that the Lord cares little for a child's promise made when she is worried. Come. Let's have no more of this nonsense. Stand and run, Abigail. I know you wish to, and it would please me to see you."

Abigail turned her eyes uncertainly up to Mama, who gave her a nod and a prod with her hand.

Abby grinned. She stood and took a deep breath. Then, lifting her skirts above her knees, she began to race. The grass and the ground flew by her in a blur. She felt ready to take off as her heart lifted, and she shouted for joy. Farther and farther she ran, until, tired and breathing hard, she stopped.

She turned and saw Mama at a great distance, waving and smiling. Just then a cloud passed overhead, blocking the sun for a minute. Abigail felt a chill. Mama seemed so far away, and the world seemed suddenly so cold. A sense of foreboding filled her, and she couldn't help but wonder, in spite of Mama's laughing, if her mother had been wrong about her promise to the Lord. What if, by breaking her promise, Abigail had led them all to some awful and terrible disaster? Standing there in the now dark and chilly air, Abigail was almost certain she had.

nine

Several weeks later, Mama, now fully recovered, prepared to do the laundry. Abigail and Dorothy carried loads of soiled garments outside to Mama, whose hands were deep in a large wooden bucket of soapy water. Dorothy began rinsing and wringing the garments, and Abigail laid them to dry in the sun. They were hard at work when Grandpappy came up the road to see them.

"Hannah," he said, "leave the washing to your daughters. I must speak to you in private."

Grandpappy would not look at them, and his clothes were askew, as if he had dressed in a hurry that day. Abigail's heart quickened.

Mama dropped the garment she had been scrubbing into the soapy water and nodded for Abigail to take over. Abby moved to do as her mother asked, but she did so quietly, hoping to hear what Grandpappy had come to say. She stole a quick glance at Dorothy beside her, who also seemed to be concentrating in order to hear.

But Grandpappy spoke in a low whisper. Abigail could hear nothing, yet she saw her mother's eyes widen.

Then Grandpappy left, without so much as a good-bye. Mama came and took the dirty garment back from Abby.

"I've got it now, Bear," she said.

"What did Grandpappy want, Mama?" Franny called out. She was sitting on the doorstep, churning butter.

"Keep your mind on your work, Franny," Mama called back to her, "and not on your grandfather."

Mama bent back over the washing tub. In a voice so soft that Abigail could barely hear it, Mama spoke to them.

"Joseph Ballard has sent for the girls from Salem Village who claim to be tormented by the devil," she said. "He believes that his wife's illness is a sign of the devil's work, so the girls have been sent for to see if the devil is amongst us. Grandpappy has tried in vain to stop them coming, but no one would listen."

"Could it be so, Mama?" Dorothy asked. "Could the devil be the cause of Mistress Ballard's illness? She has been ill for a long time."

Mama shrugged. "I know not, Dorothy. But do you believe that one amongst us is doing the devil's work?"

Abigail thought back to the harsh words said to her on the Sabbath after her day in the stocks.

"Perhaps Goody Sprague," she said, smiling.

Dorothy giggled.

But Mama gave them both a sharp look. "Words such as those are the very reason Grandpappy believes the girls are accusing so many in Salem Village. It is revenge, not the devil."

"Well then," Dorothy said sensibly, "the girls will find nothing here. They have no argument with anyone of Andover."

"I hope that is true," Mama said, sighing.

"When do the girls arrive?" Abby asked.

"On the morrow," Mama replied.

Abigail thought about these girls who had been touched by the devil. What would they look like?

Would they show signs of the devil or the witches that were tormenting them?

"Can we go see them?" Abigail asked.

"Certainly not, Abigail Faulkner," her mother said firmly. "On the morrow, we will be attending to our mending and dyeing as we do every Wednesday. Your father and Paul will see to the planting. I'll have no foolishness over these girls. There are chores to be done, and chasing after the devil is not one of them."

Abigail sighed. She almost envied the girls. She would have welcomed a ride in the summer sunshine from Salem Village to Andover. There would be no chores for *them* that day. They could sit and ride and talk the whole way over, something children were rarely allowed.

"What are you whispering about?" Franny called from the porch.

Mama turned and smiled back at her. "Nothing, little one. How is that butter?"

"'Tis slow in coming," Franny grumped, "and my arm is weary."

Mama frowned. "Your backside will be weary, Franny Faulkner, if you don't finish your churning."

She turned and handed the last of the garments to

Dorothy. "I wish to keep this from Franny and Paul," she said. "I expect you will speak naught of it to them."

Abigail and Dorothy nodded their agreement, but in her heart, Abigail wondered if the secret they kept would be quiet for long. Soon all the town would know of the girls' arrival.

The next morning, Abigail woke to a day full of sunshine and the knowledge that this was the day the girls were to arrive from Salem Village. She tried to imagine them riding over the rutted road toward Andover, their eyes troubled from their encounters with the devil and his witches. *Maybe,* she thought, *there were even marks on their arms where they had been touched by those evil hands.* She shook the thought from her head.

"Abigail," called her mother. "Do you think you are to stay abed all day?"

"I'm coming, Mama," Abby called back. She rose swiftly. The summer sunshine was pouring in through the diamond-shaped windows, making beautiful colors on the wooden floor. It hardly seemed like a day for devilry.

Abigail dressed and went down to help with the breakfast and to feed the chickens. She laughed as the animals scurried around, pecking at her feet. She lifted her face to the sunshine and smiled.

"Bear!" Mama called sharply. "You are a slow child today. Come in for breakfast and then we must tend to our mending. Paul ripped a hole in his best breeches last Sunday that seems as wide as the ocean itself."

Abigail went back inside the house.

"Mama," she asked, "do you think we could sit outside and mend? The day is so beautiful that I hate the thought of being in a dark house."

Mama smiled affectionately at her daughter. "Aye, Abby, 'tis a fine idea for today. As long as your thoughts don't wander from your chores, I think it would be a most pleasant way to do our mending."

Dorothy, who was filling the plates up with breakfast, smiled at Abigail, pleasure on her face. Franny clapped her hands with excitement.

Paul came in. "What is everyone so merry about?" he asked.

"Mama says we can sit outside to do our mending," Franny said.

Paul rolled his eyes. "I'd take one day sitting

inside doing your female chores instead of all the chores I have to do outside, sunshine or not. You have it easy every day, Franny."

"Do not," Franny said, sticking out her tongue.

"Do too," Paul said.

"Do not," Dorothy said hotly, coming to Franny's defense. "I've never seen you wring a chicken's neck and pluck its feathers, or birth a pig, or brush wool until your hands bleed trying to make it clean and fine."

"Well, I never saw you chop wood, or build a barn, or sit still in the woods hunting, unable to move at all, even when you have to go in the worst sort of way," Paul shot back.

"Enough, enough," Mama said, smiling. "Come along and eat now so you can get back to your horrible lives."

That set them all to laughing, and when Papa came in, they were still giggling. His eyes lit up when he saw them.

"And what has everyone so cheery, might I ask?" he said.

"The girls are doing their chores outside today," Paul complained.

"You may do your chores outside today too, Paul," Papa joked.

"That's a fine offer," Paul grumbled.

They all laughed at his grumpiness, until even he joined in laughing. Papa grinned at Abigail, and she couldn't help but grin back. Since that time in May, Papa had been fine. And in spite of her resentment of his fits, when Papa was fine, everything seemed right with the world.

Later, the girls sat on stools out in the sunshine, the huge basket of mending at their feet. Abigail leaned her back against the warm wood of the house. Her needle went in and out, in and out, slowly mending each rift and tear.

They worked in silence, but it was companionable. The beauty of the day surrounded them. Occasionally, Abigail let the mending fall from her hands and gazed out across the land in front of her, awash in the brilliance of summer sunshine.

It was at one such moment that she spotted Aunt Elizabeth, hurrying up the hill toward them.

"Aunt Elizabeth is coming," she said to her sisters.

"Mama," she called, for Mama had gone inside

to check the fire, "Aunt Lizzy is coming."

Mama came to the door, wiping her hands on a cloth. "Perhaps she'll stay to eat, then," Mama said, smiling. "When Paul comes in from the fields for supper, he can run and fetch Daniel to see if he'll join us. That would be most pleasant."

But as Aunt Elizabeth drew near, Abigail could see the worry on her face. Mama's smile disappeared.

"Eliza," Mama said, "what is it? You look distressed."

"Aye, sister, I am. Most terrible news has reached us, and I hurried here to give it to you," Aunt Elizabeth said. "The girls arrived from Salem Village and were taken to Mistress Ballard's house and to many others who were sick."

Mama glanced at Franny, who sat very still on her stool.

"Perhaps we should speak of this inside, Elizabeth," Mama said.

"There is no need, Hannah," Aunt Elizabeth said. "I fear everyone will know shortly. For in each house they visited, the girls did see a witch at the head and the foot of each sickbed."

Abigail turned to Dorothy, whose eyes were

wide. How was this possible? Witches in Andover? Abigail knew each and every person in her town. It did not seem possible that one of them could be a witch.

"Did they accuse anyone?" Mama asked.

"Nay," Aunt Elizabeth said, "they cannot. The names in this town are not known to them. But Reverend Barnard and Justice Bradstreet have ordered that all in the town come to the meetinghouse and present themselves to the girls. There, they believe, the girls will be able to identify those who are working with the devil and causing these illnesses."

Abigail could not believe what she was hearing. Would she and her family actually be taken to the meetinghouse and paraded in front of these girls? She had a fleeting thought of her father. Would they accuse him? No! There was no way for the girls to be aware of his fits. *Unless,* she thought, *someone told them!*

"Did not our father try to put a stop to this madness?" Mama asked, her voice rising.

"Aye," Aunt Elizabeth said. "But the townsfolk would have none of it. They believe the girls and want to know who amongst us is a witch."

"But if the girls do lie, what is to stop them from accusing innocent people here in Andover?" Mama cried.

"Nothing, sister," Aunt Elizabeth whispered. "Nothing at all."

ten

Abigail followed the others toward town. She kept her eye on Papa, but he seemed strangely calm in the midst of this storm. This morning he had even brought a newly born lamb into the house for Franny, letting her hold him and name him. It was as if it were just another ordinary day to him.

Mama walked quickly, her boots making sharp indentations in the dirt. She was angry at the wasted day, grumbling all morning about the foolishness of this meeting.

Dorothy, Paul, and Franny were frightened, though. As they approached the meetinghouse, their steps slowed, until at last it seemed to Abigail that they were like earthworms crawling toward their doom.

"Come along," Mama called back to them. "Let us be finished with this thing. There are chores to be done, and we mustn't be about wasting the whole of the day with this nonsense."

"I don't see why we have to do it at all," Dorothy whispered.

"You're just scared they'll find you out for the devil you are," Paul said with a laugh.

"If there is a devil in this family, his name begins with a *P*," Dorothy shot back.

"That's enough," Papa warned, and Paul and Dorothy grew quiet, though they knew Papa would do nothing about it if they continued to bicker.

Franny grabbed hold of Abigail's hand. "There's no devil in our family, is there, Abigail?"

Abby looked down at her sister's wide, frightened eyes.

"Surely not, Franny," Abigail said. "Would you take me for a witch?"

Franny shook her head.

"Paul then? Or Dorothy? Or little Edward?" Abigail asked.

Franny shook her head again.

"Or Mama or Papa?" Abigail questioned.

Here Franny hesitated. Abigail prayed that Franny would not hesitate like that at the meetinghouse.

Finally, Franny shook her head again.

"Then see here," Abigail said sharply. "We have naught to fear from these girls or the witches that bother them."

"What if the witches see me at the meetinghouse," Franny whispered, "and they come for me as they did for those girls from Salem Village?"

Surely that was not possible in their own meetinghouse, but even Abigail felt a slight uncertainty.

Before she could reply, they arrived. The townsfolk milled around outside, their voices low, their eyes uneasy and wary. The children were strangely silent. Abigail could not remember such a troubled feeling in the town ever before.

Mistress Stevens came toward them. "Good morrow, Mistress Faulkner," she said to Mama. "Is this not a most distressing business? To think that perhaps there are witches amongst us in Andover."

"Let us hope, Mistress Stevens," Mama said, "that there has been some mistake made here, and that the shapes these girls have seen are but shadows made in the candlelit rooms of our sick townsfolk."

"Perhaps that is true, Mistress Faulkner," Mistress Stevens replied, "but there is much happening in this town that I do find hard to explain."

At this, she turned her eyes on Abigail's father. Mama reached out and took Papa's arm, holding tightly to it. Papa smiled slightly, but said nothing.

"Perhaps you aren't looking hard enough for simple answers, Mistress Stevens," Abigail spoke up. "The Lord explains all for us if we pray hard enough."

Dorothy sucked in her breath at Abby's insolence. Mama did not reprimand her, but instead seemed to be biting her lip to keep from smiling.

Mistress Stevens bristled at the rebuke and turned from them just as the younger minister of the town, Reverend Barnard, came out onto the steps of the meetinghouse.

"Abigail," Mama whispered.

"I know," Abby sighed. "I shouldn't have said it, but I couldn't help myself."

Mama laughed softly.

"Let us all proceed inside," Reverend Barnard said to the townspeople.

Aunt Elizabeth had come and stood beside

Abigail. Uncle Daniel was with her. "Where is your grandfather?"

Abigail shook her head. She, too, wondered why he was not there on this most awful of days.

As they had done so many times, the family entered the meetinghouse. Today, however, Abigail paused on the threshold of the house of the Lord. Would she see hell and damnation today? Would the devil see evil in her and take her as his servant too?

"Do not tarry so, Abby," Paul hissed at her.

Abigail started, realizing that she had been blocking the entrance to the meetinghouse like some fainthearted coward. Lifting her head high, she followed her family up the aisle and sat down on the hard wooden pew.

When at last they brought the girls in, a murmur arose from the townsfolk. They craned their necks to get a better look at the girls who had been touched by the devil. Even Abigail rose from her seat, until she felt Mama's hand on her arm, tugging at her so that she would sit down.

The girls looked normal. Their hair was neatly

brushed, their clothes clean and tear-free, their faces unmarked by the devil. Then suddenly they began to cry out, to moan and tear at their hair and pinch their arms. Abigail jumped at the suddenness of it all, and Franny, beside her, began to shake. The congregants shifted uneasily in their places.

"Mama," Franny whimpered, "why do these girls act so?"

"They say they are tormented by the devil, pinched by him, and made to suffer by him," Mama whispered. "They claim that they are tortured until his witches lay their hands upon them. Then and only then does their suffering end."

"Is it so, Mama?" Paul whispered loudly across the aisle from the men's side of the meetinghouse.

"It's nonsense," Papa said, bouncing Edward on his knee.

Mama nodded her head in agreement. "In truth, Paul," she whispered back across to him, "I believe their stories to be false."

Abigail stared in fascination as the girls were led to the front of the room, moaning and groaning and crying out. Was the devil there? Maybe Mama and

Papa were wrong, and the devil was indeed in the meetinghouse sitting somewhere near to her.

Then, from the corner of her eye, she saw Grandpappy. He had come in a side door and gone to the back of the meetinghouse. Abigail could see he was troubled, yet he said nothing, only stood and watched as the younger minister conducted the meeting. Abigail remembered her grandfather's words about believing that the girls were only playing a game.

Still, she had to admit, if they were playing, their acting was skillful. The girls' moans grew incredibly loud, and Abigail reached up and covered her ears, her eyes still fastened on them. Mama gave her a sharp look, and Abigail lowered her hands to her lap. But her heart beat rapidly, and her palms were sweaty. She hated the unaccustomed feeling of fright, but the girls' shrieks were gruesome.

"I stand before ye with Ann Putnam and Mary Walcott of Salem Village," said Reverend Barnard. "These girls, having late been touched by the devil, have come to seek out his presence in Andover. Because we are a God-fearing town, we do most urgently wish to rid our town of any devilry, should it exist. Therefore, in all fairness, we will choose at random from this congregation, blindfold them, and bring them forth to see if any of us are a witch."

With this, Elder Stevens came around to the first of the pews. He motioned to one of the townspeople to step forward, and then placed a blindfold over the man's eyes so that if the man were consorting with the devil, he would be unable to turn an evil eye on the girls when he touched them.

Watching the man being led forward, Abigail felt hope return. If the test was to be random, maybe they would not be chosen at all.

The deacons came and stood by different pews, motioning for first one and then another to rise up and present himself or herself to the girls. Abigail watched as various townsfolk walked to the front of the meetinghouse. One by one, Elder Stevens blindfolded each person, then took his or her hand and drew it toward Ann Putnam or Mary Walcott.

At first, nothing happened. The girls continued to twist and moan. But then it was Mistress Osgood's turn to stretch out her hand, and suddenly, Mary Walcott was still.

The quiet astounded everyone. Abigail stared at Mistress Osgood. Was she a witch? How was this possible? She made coverlets that she said were inspired by God. They were known to be works of art. Abigail herself had spent many afternoons learning to stitch with gentle Mistress Osgood.

"But I am innocent. I am not a witch!" Mistress Osgood cried as her blindfold was removed. Justice Bradstreet nodded for her to follow him.

"Please," she begged, "let me take another turn. Something is amiss here! I am no witch!"

Reverend Barnard nodded. Again, Mistress Osgood's hand was drawn toward one of the girls, and again, quiet settled in the meetinghouse. Mistress Osgood began to weep. Abigail was amazed.

But more were to follow. Samuel Wardwell quieted one of the girls, and so did William Barker. The girls were quieted by many of the townsfolk, as if these people had it in their power to end the girls' suffering!

Abigail looked at these people, these neighbors. Had they been living right next to her and yet working with the devil? Or were the girls lying, choosing victims at random? Did the girls speak the truth or did Grandpappy? Why did he not say something, if he believed they were lying?

Abigail turned to look for her grandfather. He stood quietly at the back, his eyes fixed on the events occurring at the front of the meetinghouse. He seemed barely able to breathe.

"This is absurd," Mama said. "These people are not witches."

Abigail saw that a deacon was now approaching them. His face was pale but stern, and she knew at once that they were not to be passed over. Even the minister's family must take its turn. Especially the minister's family. The deacon nodded toward both sides of the aisle.

"The whole family?" Mama asked indignantly.

He nodded again.

Abigail rose with the rest of her family. She looked at Papa. He twitched slightly. *Please, Papa,* Abby prayed, *stay well.*

"Walk proudly, children," Mama whispered.

She followed the others toward the front of the meetinghouse. Franny went first, whimpering as they pulled her hand toward the girls, her eyes blindfolded. The girls continued to twist and groan and cry.

Next was Paul, and then Dorothy, neither of whom caused a change in either girl. Then it was Abigail's turn. The blindfold was placed over her eyes, and she could see nothing. She felt Elder Stevens take her hand firmly in his. Abigail's lip quivered. Yet why should she be frightened? She was not a witch.

She drew a deep breath and pushed her hand out to touch one of the girls.

Nothing. Nothing happened. The girl continued her moaning and crying.

Abigail's breathing returned to normal as she was led away and the blindfold taken from her eyes. But then she realized that Mama and Papa had yet to go. She turned to watch.

Mama reached out boldly and touched Mary Walcott. Nothing.

Papa, too, reached out on his own and touched Ann Putnam. Ann's cries lessened for a moment. Abigail heard Dorothy draw in her breath, but then

Ann cried out, even louder than before. Papa was passed on. Their family had made it through the test.

Abigail turned to look at the ones who had quieted the girls, the ones who had been accused of being witches. Standing in the corner with Justice Bradstreet, who was signing petitions for their arrest, were more than half a dozen people, their eyes betraying their bewilderment and dismay.

Abigail slipped her hand inside her mother's and squeezed hard. Mama squeezed back. Yet Abigail was still uneasy. *If there had been so many witches living in this tiny town,* she wondered, *how had the town of Andover ever had one normal day? Was it possible for this much evil to exist in so small a community? Or were these good neighbors and friends only caught up in some awful game?*

Abigail was grateful that they were not among those who must now prove their innocence. The danger for the Faulkner family was past. That was truly what she believed.

eleven

At first Mama refused to listen

to Abigail and her brother and sisters begging for news of the accused. She refused to discuss the gossip that was being told around the village. She wouldn't let the chores wait for even an hour so they could visit the families of the accused and find out what was happening to them in prison as they awaited their trial.

But after two weeks, even Mama seemed unable to contain her curiosity about the events in the village.

"Paul," she called one day, "run on down to the meetinghouse and see if you can find your grandfather. Pray tell him that we would be most happy to have him join us for supper."

Dorothy and Abigail looked at each other but said nothing.

"Abby," Franny whispered, "if Grandpappy comes, will he have news of the witches?"

"I believe so," Abigail said.

Her sister went back to her mending, but Abigail could see that her hands were trembling. Since the day in the meetinghouse when Franny had been forced to touch the hand of Ann Putnam, her sister had lived in fear that the witches of Andover would soon come to get her.

"Fear not, Franny," Abigail said. "Grandpappy will not bring the witches with him, only news of them." She imagined Grandpappy climbing up the hill from town, dozens of witches in tow behind him, and she laughed at the thought.

"I don't see what is so funny," Franny muttered, "just because you are not frightened of the devil."

"Oh, I am frightened of the devil, sister," Dorothy put in. "I just do not believe the devil works with Mistress Osgood."

"But if he does," Abigail said, smiling, "then the devil will be guaranteed a most beautiful coverlet in which to wrap himself up."

Dorothy and Abigail broke out into giggles at the

thought of Mistress Osgood stitching the devil a coverlet.

"You should not have such sport at Mistress Osgood's expense," Franny said softly, her hands shaking. "When I think of her now, I think of her in that jail in Salem Town."

This quieted Abigail and Dorothy. The Salem Town Prison, in Salem Town proper, was a few miles from Salem Village, where the accused girls lived. It was said to be a dark and dank place, full of rancid smells and all kinds of horrible things. Abigail was truly sorry for Mistress Osgood.

"You are quite right, Franny," Dorothy said quietly. "It was unthinking of Abigail and me to forget that fact."

Several minutes later, Paul came in the door, his face flushed from having run downhill to the meetinghouse and back. "Grandpappy says he will be here for supper, but that he may be late and we must not wait for him."

"Thank you, Paul," Mama said. "Let us hurry, girls. Papa will be in from the fields soon. Dorothy, leave your spinning and see to the fire."

A cry sounded from upstairs.

"Abigail, please fetch down Edward for me, and see to his changing should he need it," Mama bade her. "It is most difficult for me to manage the stairs these days."

Abigail nodded, looking at Mama's swelling belly. In the last few weeks, the baby had begun to move about. Mama had let Abigail lay her hand on her belly and feel the gentle tapping of her new brother or sister.

Abigail loved that feeling. "I believe he is telling me good morrow," Abigail had said.

Mama had laughed. "He or she says good morrow in a gentle fashion now, Bear. But give it a few more weeks and this baby will be drumming out its greetings upon my belly. I remember well how you pressed upon me, and how I rubbed like this to quiet you." Mama had rubbed where the baby had fluttered.

Abigail had smiled, glad that even with the new baby, Mama remembered carrying her. Mama had then kissed her on the forehead and risen to tend to the fire.

Now Abigail hurried up the stairs to take care of Edward. He was just waking, stirring wildly in his cradle, which was growing too small for him.

"Just in time, Edward. You shall be out of this cradle and into an underbed," Abigail said, smiling at him.

She picked him up and put her nose to his behind. Abigail groaned. Edward would need changing, and that was a task she hated.

From downstairs, she heard Papa come in for supper. Then she heard her grandfather's voice. She wondered why he was so early when he had told Paul that he would be late.

Quickly, Abby finished changing Edward, then lifted him into her arms, though he squirmed to be let down. She hurried back down the stairs.

At the bottom of the steps, she stopped. The kitchen was deathly quiet. There were tears in Mama's eyes, and Dorothy had her hand over her mouth. Papa was staring at the newly sanded floor.

"What?" Abigail cried. "What has happened?"

Edward struggled against her, and Abigail put him on the floor to toddle over to Mama.

Grandpappy turned toward Abigail. "Your aunt Elizabeth has been accused of being a witch. Justice Bradstreet signed the warrant for her arrest this morning."

Abigail stared. Aunt Elizabeth? Everyone loved Aunt Elizabeth. It was simply not possible that her aunt could be a witch. Abigail now knew with all her heart that the girls were lying.

"Aunt Elizabeth is no witch, Grandpappy," Franny said.

"Of course not," Grandpappy said irritably. "It is but the anger of those girls that is at work here."

"At whom are they angry?" Papa asked.

"At me," Grandpappy said. "I have been busy these weeks speaking out against the girls, trying to free our people, whom I know to be innocent. Now it seems I am to know the price of telling the truth."

Grandpappy sank into a chair. "My daughter!" he railed. "Those lying girls have turned on my daughter and have had her dragged off to jail in Salem Town."

Grandpappy's shoulders slumped, and with horror, Abigail saw that her strong grandfather was crying. If *he* had no hope, no answer, it seemed to Abby that all must be lost.

Mama rose from her chair and went to Grandpappy. "Come. Tears will do Eliza no good, Father. You and I know that she is no witch. What we must do now is find a way to prove this to the town. But first, we must eat. Full bellies make strong minds."

There was a knock at the door, and Uncle Daniel came in. His face was ashen. "They have taken her," he said.

Mama nodded. "Come eat with us, Daniel," she said. "We will think of a way to free Elizabeth."

"I know not if I can eat," Uncle Daniel muttered, sinking onto a stool by the fire. Papa went and put his hand on Daniel's shoulder.

Grandpappy shook his head. "I am sorry, Daniel," he said. "I should not have spoken out. I should have been quiet, and perhaps this would not have happened."

"Nonsense, Father," Mama snapped. "Someone must end the lies these girls are telling. If no one stands up for the truth, then the truth ceases to be. We shall free Elizabeth and the rest of this town from the lies of those girls. Come, let us eat. Then we will talk."

Abigail went to help her mother with the supper. But the thought of their earlier laughter at Mistress

Osgood's expense soured Abigail's appetite now that she knew Aunt Elizabeth to be sharing the same fate. She looked at the dessert she had made, bread pudding and molasses. It was her favorite, and yet she felt her stomach churn.

"Boston," Mama said, once the meal was finished. "We must make the trip to Boston. It will take a day, but we can appeal to the governor there, Father. Mayhap he has not heard what is happening here and will see reason. He may order an end to this madness."

Grandpappy nodded, a ghost of a smile coming to his face. "'Tis a fine idea, daughter. We will go on the morrow."

But Mama and Grandpappy's trip was for nothing. The governor listened to all they said but was unwilling to get involved.

The trials for their neighbors began soon after Mama and Grandpappy returned. Mama refused to allow the family to attend.

"I will not have my family neglecting this household and giving their attention to those disturbed girls," Mama said.

"But Mama, what if the girls are right about some

people?" Franny said. "What if there are witches amongst us? We know that Aunt Elizabeth is not one, but does this mean that none exist?"

"We will do our chores without further nonsense," Mama replied.

Her mother had not answered Franny's question, and Abigail wondered if perhaps even Mama was not sure of the answer.

There was a knock at the open door.

"Hannah?" Uncle Daniel stood, peering into the house.

"Come in, Daniel," Mama said. "Do you have news of Eliza?"

Uncle Daniel came in quickly and took Mama's hand. There were dark circles under his eyes. "Aye, I have seen her," he said. "She fares well enough in that awful place. But I fear there is more bad news. Sarah Phelps has been to see the magistrates. She claims to be tormented by witches of this town, and she means to accuse someone."

"We have naught to fear from Sarah Phelps," Mama said.

Abigail exchanged glances with Dorothy. Had Mama forgotten why Sarah had left their household?

She could easily remind everyone of Papa's fits. And Sarah could mention to the magistrates the day that Mama had sat up so abruptly in her sickbed and cried out. While Abigail now knew it was nothing more than the fever, would Sarah construe it to be the work of the devil?

"This thing grows worse daily," Uncle Daniel said. He dropped Mama's hand and paced the room, running his fingers through his hair. "The trials are most awful to behold, with the accusers moaning and groaning and screaming for the accused to stop tormenting them. There our neighbors stand, wringing their hands in terror, not knowing what to say. They are confused, Hannah. And truly, I am confused too. Have we all gone mad?"

Mama went and put her arm around Uncle Daniel. "Come sit with me, Daniel. You must rest your mind. These days are troubled, I know. But we work hourly to end this madness and to free Elizabeth. I am certain we will succeed."

Dorothy came to Abigail's side.

"I fear for Mama, Abby," Dorothy whispered. "She does not remember what Sarah Phelps witnessed that day. Should we tell her?"

"Nay, Dorothy," Abigail said. "Let us not trouble Mama unduly. Instead, let us pray with all our might that Sarah Phelps is accusing someone other than Mama or Papa."

Yet in the morning, Constable Ballard and Justice Bradstreet came to their door.

Abigail stood behind Mama and Papa. Her prayers hadn't mattered. They had come.

"We are here," Justice Bradstreet said, as he stood tall and stern in the warm summer air, "for the two witches that lie within this house."

Mama stepped boldly forward. "Witches?" she said scornfully, her back erect. "Come, William. Come, Dudley. We are neighbors. You know my husband and I are not witches."

"You have not been accused, Hannah," Justice Bradstreet replied, "nor your husband."

"Well, if not us," Papa asked, bewildered, "then who?"

"Abigail Faulkner and Dorothy Faulkner," Constable Ballard replied. "They have been accused."

twelve

Abigail felt as if the ground beneath her were swaying back and forth. Had she heard Constable Ballard correctly? Had he accused her of being a witch?

Papa laughed. "Pray, what is this, William?" he said. "Surely you jest. Are you but having a bit of sport with us?"

Constable Ballard shook his head. "I fear not, Francis. Sarah Phelps has accused them."

Mama reached out and pulled Abigail and Dorothy to her.

"Mama?" Franny said in a high, thin voice. "What is happening?"

"Franny," Mama said, "stay behind me, child."

Papa's face hardened. He took a step toward Justice Bradstreet, his hands clenched at his sides. Paul moved up beside him, and Abigail saw the anger in her brother's face.

"Surely, sir, you don't mean to suggest that Abigail and Dorothy serve the devil?" Papa's voice was loud. "They are but children."

Abigail stared. Never had she seen her father so angry or firm.

"'Tis not for me to decide, Francis," Justice Bradstreet said. "I am simply serving the arrest."

"An arrest for *children!*" Mama cried. "*Children!* Think on it, Dudley. Is there not some part of you that knows this to be wrong?"

"Hannah," Justice Bradstreet said, "surely you are aware that I do not think your children are witches. But I must do my job."

"You will have difficulty, then, sir, doing your job today or on the morrow," Papa said, his voice strong. "You will not take my children. I forbid it!"

Dorothy gasped.

Justice Bradstreet stepped up to Papa and looked him directly in the eye. "They have been accused,

Francis," he said. "They will have their chance to prove their innocence at trial. Unless, of course, you mean to defy the laws of this community."

Abigail saw her father look at Justice Bradstreet's stern face and his fists that were also clenched, as if for battle.

Papa's face fell, and he stepped away. Abigail wanted to scream at him, to yell and tell him to do something, to be strong for them. Was that small confrontation all Papa was to do?

Constable Ballard brought some rope. On the other side of Mama, Dorothy began to whimper. Franny was crying. From upstairs, Edward's wails could be heard.

"You will take me before you shall take my children, William," Mama said, pulling Abigail and Dorothy in tighter.

Constable Ballard sighed. "Hannah, I truly wish I did not need to do this. But Sarah Phelps has claimed that these girls are tormenting her, and it is my duty to arrest them on charges of witchcraft. If they be no witches, they can prove it in court."

"And what happens to them before their day in

court?" Mama asked, her voice rising, becoming shrill with panic. "Surely you do not mean to condemn my children to the prison in Salem Town, that most terrible of places? Surely they can remain somewhere here in Andover until they can prove their ill-use at the hands of Sarah Phelps!"

Justice Bradstreet sighed too. "I fear not, Hannah. The law is the law."

Constable Ballard began to approach the girls.

Paul stepped in front of them. "You heard my mother," he said. "You'll not take my sisters."

Constable Ballard smiled. "Come, Paul. Step away."

Paul shook his head. Justice Bradstreet came up behind him and pushed him to the side. Paul lost his balance and fell hard to the ground, scraping his hand. Abby wanted to hug him for trying to protect them.

"Are you all right, son?" Papa said, holding out a hand to help Paul up.

Paul stared at him. "What matters that, Father?" he said. "Abigail and Dorothy are to be taken."

"Go inside, Paul," Papa said, looking not at his

children now but at the ground. "Do not interfere."

"That is always your solution," Paul muttered, wiping the blood from his hand and scowling.

"Enough," Papa said, a tear running down his cheek. "Go inside."

Paul looked at his sisters, frowning with frustration, then he went into the house.

Constable Ballard reached out to take Dorothy. Abigail watched as if in a dream.

"Nay!" Mama cried. "Nay! You will not take my children."

In reaching out to protect Dorothy, Mama let go of Abby. Justice Bradstreet snatched Abigail up, forcing her hands in front of her and tying them together. The rope was tight, and it dug into her wrists.

"Nay!" Mama screamed, seeing Abigail being hustled toward the back of the wagon. "Nay! They are but children!"

Now that Mama's focus was on Abigail, Constable Ballard swiftly reached out and pulled Dorothy from her.

"Nay!" Mama screamed again.

Abigail was lifted up onto Constable Ballard's wagon. Her stomach churned, yet her mind remained strangely calm. She watched as Mama beat her fists on the constable's back, and Abigail felt as if she were someone else as Mama fell to the ground, weeping.

Dorothy was lifted up next, screaming and kicking. She stared at Abigail as if she had lost her mind.

"How can you just sit there?" Dorothy cried. "Do you not understand what has happened to us?"

As quickly as the detachment had come, it was over. Abigail's stomach was now tossing and turning so violently that she had to turn her head over the side of the wagon to be sick.

"I will follow you to Salem Town," Papa called to them as Constable Ballard climbed into the front of the wagon. "I will bring the money necessary that you should be in comfort there."

Lowering her head to wipe her mouth on her bent knees, Abigail felt anger well inside her. This was her father's solution?

Mama rose from the ground. She screamed and

ran to the wagon, trying to swing herself up on it.

"Stop, Hannah," Justice Bradstreet cried out, "or you too shall end up in Salem Town Prison and be of no help to these children."

Mama stared at him and then gave up trying to climb into the back of the wagon. She reached into the wagon and touched Dorothy's cheek and then Abigail's. "Papa will ride with you now," she said. "I will send Paul to tell Grandpappy what has happened. Aunt Elizabeth will be there, and I shall do everything in my power to free you."

Dorothy continued to cry, but Abigail, seeing the fear in Mama's face, decided that the best thing to do was to be brave for her.

"Worry not, Mama," Abigail said. "I will be strong, and I will take care of Dorothy."

"You are not witches," Mama said, her voice shaking. "Remember that you are innocent and shall soon be free.

"I love you," she added in a whisper.

Abigail heard the crack of the whip, and the horses moved forward. Dorothy buried her face in her skirts, but Abigail watched as Mama's figure grew smaller and smaller, until at last she could see her no more.

She remembered envying the girls from Salem Village their sunny ride to Andover. She had gotten her wish. She too was making a trip. *But to what?* she wondered.

The ride was eighteen miles, and the sun was hot on Abby's back as they rode along the rutted road. The wagon swayed from side to side, throwing her and Dorothy back and forth. Abby wished for the ride to be over, yet at the same time, she knew the end meant the Salem Town jail.

Papa had saddled a horse and came galloping up behind them. He rode next to them now, saying nothing. Abigail knew he meant well, but the truth of his weakness washed over her, and his presence brought her no comfort. She knew there was little he was capable of doing to help them.

Dorothy spent the ride hunched over, crying. Abigail wished she could think of something to say that would quiet and reassure her sister, but she could think of nothing.

At last they began to see small farms and houses from which smoke curled lazily in the warm summer air.

"We are near to Salem Town, girls," Papa said. "Prepare yourselves."

As they entered the town, Abigail looked about her. In spite of her fear, she was curious, for she had never before been in such a big town with so many people. The wagon took a turn, moving east toward the harbor. As they approached the ocean, Abigail took a deep breath of the salt air, amazed at its smell.

The street widened, and suddenly the wagon came upon the wharf. The scene before them was full of life and activity.

Ships were at the dock. Wagons were unloading. The sound of iron against an anvil rang out. People hustled and bustled about.

"Look!" someone cried, pointing toward Abigail and her sister. "Is it witches from afar?"

Instantly, everyone moved away from the wagon, looking in fear at Dorothy and Abigail. Someone picked up a stone and hurled it at them. It bounced harmlessly against the wagon's side but caused Abigail to jump.

"Stand away from the wagon and let us pass," Constable Ballard yelled out.

"I'll stand away," one man jeered. "You'll not see me near a witch."

At this, the townsfolk began to boo and hiss at the sisters. Dorothy covered her eyes with her tied hands. But Abigail continued to look out at the crowd. How could they act like this toward them? They had not even been proven guilty!

"Look how she stares," one woman cried out. "She means us evil."

"Abigail," Papa whispered, "lower your eyes, or I fear there will be trouble. Please. I do not want you hurt."

Abigail did as he asked, but her heart was filled with fury at these people who thought she was guilty without even hearing what she had to say in her defense, and at Papa for refusing to let her fight back the only way she could. And she was angry at herself for complying with his wishes and not defending herself.

At last, the wagon came to a stop at a massive wooden building by the water. Constable Ballard came down from the wagon and walked to the back to help Abigail and Dorothy to the ground.

Abigail's heart quickened as she looked up at the forbidding building. She took a deep breath of fresh air, as she knew it could be one of her last for a long time. Then, following Dorothy, she climbed the steps of the prison.

thirteen

Constable Ballard knocked on
the large wooden door. "I have prisoners to deliver,"
he called.

They waited outside for what seemed an incredibly
long time, until at last a key was heard. The door
swung open, creaking loudly in protest.

A dour-faced old man met them, his back bowed,
his hair greasy. "Let me see the arrest form," he said.
"I'll take no more unless the form is signed."

Constable Ballard handed over the arrest papers,
and the old man squinted to see them. Finally he
sighed. "Don't know where they mean me to put
them. The jail's full up with witches."

Abigail heard his words with dismay. Until that

moment, she had been so absorbed in the thought of herself and Dorothy in this terrible place that it had not occurred to her there could be *real* witches in the prison.

The old man peered out at them. "Is the devil now turning children to his work?" he asked.

"So they have been accused," Constable Ballard replied.

The old man cackled, showing a mouth with hardly any teeth. "Come in then, young witches," he said, "and see your new lodgings."

He stepped back from the door, and the constable nodded for Dorothy, Abigail, and Papa to enter. Dorothy shrank back, but Abigail walked through the doorway with her shoulders back. She blinked as she entered, for the outside had been bright with sunshine, but inside, the light was dim.

There came a terrible odor from somewhere down the hall in front of them. Papa pulled out a cloth and put it to his nose. Dorothy began to cough as she came and stood next to Abigail. Even Constable Ballard flinched as he stepped in behind them, though he must have been there several times before.

"Whence comes that stench?" Dorothy asked the jailer between coughs.

"From below," said the old man. "Witches have a smell after being here for a time."

Dorothy looked as if she were going to faint. Papa put out an arm to steady her.

"I want my daughters in the most comfortable cell you have to offer," Papa said.

The old man smiled wickedly. "Of course, sir. It will cost you, though."

Papa nodded. "I am aware of the cost. My sister-in-law is already here."

"And who might she be?" the old man inquired.

"Elizabeth Johnson," Papa said.

The old man nodded. "Aye," he said. "I know of her. Her husband does pay most handsomely for her keep." He smiled at them. "I am at the end of life's time," he added. "Had I but known how wealthy I was to become for the keeping of witches, I daresay I might have enjoyed my youth a bit more."

"I don't believe the Faulkners share the joy at your good fortune," Constable Ballard said sharply, "especially since it is at their expense."

The old man shrugged. "It is no concern of mine that they must pay for their upkeep. The law is the law."

He turned to Abigail's father. "Sir, do I presume you mean to have your children quartered as your sister-in-law has been?"

"Aye," Papa said, "and if possible, I would mean to have my daughters housed with their aunt."

The jailer laughed again. "Anything is possible, sir. Anything for a price."

He turned and grabbed a ring of keys from the wall. "Come, then," he said. "Let me show you to your quarters."

This was it, then, Abigail thought. *The end of my freedom.* She turned and looked outside to see the sunshine one last time. Constable Ballard looked at her, his hand on the door.

"Good-bye," he said, bowing slightly.

Then he turned toward Papa. "Francis," he said, nodding to her father. Her father did not reply. Constable Ballard left them, the door clicking softly behind him.

"Let's be about it, then," the jailer said.

Abigail turned to follow the jailer. As she did, Dorothy's hand slipped inside hers. Abigail looked into her sister's eyes. They were in this together now.

As they walked, the hall began to narrow, and the smell of the place grew even stronger. Dorothy let out a little squeak, and Abigail squeezed her hand tighter. Papa tried to grab onto Dorothy's other hand, but the hallway was too narrow for three.

They arrived at a flight of stone stairs and began to descend. The sound of moaning rose up from below. Abigail slipped on a stair, but Papa caught her from behind.

Damp, cold air washed over them. Though it was summer, the Salem Town Prison seemed unaware of it.

At last they reached the ground floor. The stench was overpowering, and the voices and moans loud in Abigail's ear. They passed one cell and then another.

Abigail looked in horror. People were in cells so small that it was necessary for the prisoners to stand as there was no room for lying down. Water pooled on the stone floor. Moss grew along the walls.

"Tarry a moment, please!" a man cried out, shuffling

toward them from the back of his cell. When he reached the door, Abigail was shocked to see that his legs had been loosely chained to the back wall.

"Please, for the love of God, grant me some food," the man begged.

"I'll grant you more food when your family has paid, Goodman Hawkins, and not before," the jailer growled.

"Dear Lord," Dorothy breathed, "why is that man chained to the wall?"

"All witches are chained," the jailer said. "It prevents them from flying away at night to do harm in Salem Town."

"Are we to be chained, then?" Dorothy asked, her voice choked.

"Aye," the jailer said. "'Tis the law."

At last they came to a stop outside a large but dirty and dingy cell.

"Elizabeth Johnson," the jailer called. "You have guests."

A dark figure rose from the dimness deep in the cell and moved toward them. It was Aunt Elizabeth, but she looked so different. Her hair hung in dirty strands about her face, her body was thin and wasted, and her eyes were blank, nearly lifeless.

"Aunt Elizabeth!" Abigail cried out.

"Eliza," Papa said softly, "what has happened to you?"

She stared at the three of them, then looked at the jailer. Finally, her eyes turned to them again, and this time, she seemed to recognize them.

"Francis?" she said, her voice but a whisper. "Abigail? Dorothy? Why have you come?"

"The girls have been accused, Elizabeth," Papa said, stepping near to the bars of the cell.

"Good Lord, nay," Aunt Elizabeth moaned. "Are they to turn on children now?"

"Go no closer, Master Faulkner," the jailer said. "Visitors are to stay apart from those accused."

He took out his ring of keys. "Move back," he instructed Aunt Elizabeth, who did as she was told.

The door swung open. "Enter, children," he said.

Abigail turned to her father, her stomach churning again. Dorothy was in his embrace, her shoulders shaking with her sobs.

"Enough, enough," the jailer said. "I haven't got all day to be about waiting on your good-byes."

Dorothy moved back to let Abigail into her father's embrace. He put his arms about her, and she leaned her cheek against his chest. She wished with every fiber of her being that he could somehow save them, but she knew that to be impossible.

"God keep you, Abigail," Papa said, kissing her forehead. "Remember that I love you." Abigail looked up into his eyes and saw the love there, but she also saw an anxiousness to leave this dark and gloomy place. It was more than he could bear.

"Aye, Papa," Abigail said with a bitterness she could not hide. She took Dorothy's hand and went to enter the cell, when suddenly she saw many other shapes in the darkness.

"Good Lord," Dorothy said. "How many are housed here?"

"I am uncertain," the jailer said. "But you'll be at your leisure to find out."

Then he gave Dorothy and Abigail a prod, and they entered the cell. Aunt Elizabeth held open her arms and hugged them to her, but her hug was weak and her body and breath sour.

The jailer came up behind them and before Abigail could think about it, he had clasped leg irons to her ankles. She looked to where her chains were attached to the cell wall.

"Guard them, Elizabeth," Papa said, tears now at his eyes. "Guard them until we can end this madness."

"Aye, Francis," Aunt Elizabeth said, looking up, but her voice was faint. "I shall do as best I can, though I must tell you that in this place it will be most difficult. As you see, the conditions are hard."

"Enough," the jailer growled irritably. "You are lucky, mistress, for your conditions. They are roomier than many."

Aunt Elizabeth's eyes widened with fright. "'Tis true, sir," she said quickly. "You do treat us most kindly."

The jailer reached out for the door and swung it closed. The metal clang rang out and echoed in the walled prison.

"Now," the jailer said, motioning to Papa, who had turned his head from them. "Come, sir. Let us see to my payment."

The jailer chuckled as he walked away, his laughter bouncing off the stone walls, sounding as if the devil himself lived within.

fourteen

Abigail listened as the foot-steps of Papa and the jailer faded down the stone hallway. As they passed one cell after another, the occupants let out moans or cries for help. But when at last they mounted the stairs, the prison grew silent. The jailer had taken his torch with him, and the space, lit only by a few tallow candles that smoked and smelled of animal fat, was even gloomier and darker than before.

Abigail pressed her eyes tightly shut, then opened them, allowing herself to adjust to the darkness. In the back of the cell, she could see several rough-hewn planks of wood set into the wall. Seven or so dark shapes were huddled on the floor and on the planks.

Close by, a woman rose, her face black with dirt. She stared with hard eyes at Abigail and Dorothy. "I'll not share my bed with them, Elizabeth," she said. "You must make room for them yourself."

"Aye," came many muttered voices.

"So I shall," Aunt Elizabeth said, lifting her chin slightly and showing for a moment the proud, lovely woman she been before she came here. "I have plenty of room to give my nieces. You needn't trouble yourselves to share your space."

"Good," the woman said, spitting onto the floor.

Aunt Elizabeth took Abigail's hand and then Dorothy's. "Come," she said. "My cot is back here. You must be weary after the hard trip from Andover."

Abigail went to follow her aunt, but the leg irons were heavy, and she stumbled as she made her way to the back of the dark cell. Beside her, Dorothy stumbled too, and she began to cry again.

"Cry all you want," another woman said into the darkness. "It'll do you no good in here."

"Give her the time to cry," a softer voice answered. "Those tears are all she'll have for a while."

Abigail could hear the voices, but the light was so bad in the cell that she could not see the women at the back of the cell fully, only an eye here, a chin there, parts caught by the weak candlelight. Her aunt had stopped beside a plank, indicating that the girls could sit down.

"Pay them no attention," Aunt Elizabeth said.

Abigail dragged herself to the bed and sat. The straw on the plank gave off a terrible odor. Dorothy sat down, too, and then let out a scream and jumped up.

"Aunt Lizzy," she cried, "I have been bitten."

The women all laughed, and Aunt Elizabeth nodded. "There are a good many bedbugs in the straw," she said. "It is rarely replaced. And soon your hair will grow lousy, I fear, for there is little water for washing."

Dorothy moaned and sagged against Aunt Elizabeth. But to Abigail the lice and the bedbugs were mere annoyances. What upset her most was the darkness and stillness of the cell.

"Aunt Elizabeth," Abigail said, "what occupies your days here?"

Aunt Elizabeth smiled and sat down next to Abigail. "Abby," she said, "remember the days at home when you wished with all your heart to be rid of your chores?"

Abigail nodded. Many mornings she had rolled over, wishing only for her warm bed and a longer sleep, no kneading of bread, no stirring of soap, no cleaning of wool, nor spinning of cloth.

"Here your wish will be granted," Aunt Elizabeth said. "But I fear that is exactly what makes this place most intolerable. There is nothing to do all the day but wait and hope for your next meal, if you should be lucky enough to have money to pay for one, or for a visitor, or for one of us to at last be given our trial."

"Small hope that offers," one woman said. "Not one of us has been found innocent. The trial does but prepare us to be sentenced to die if we deny being a witch, or be imprisoned in here forever for confessing to witchcraft."

"Has anyone here confessed?" Dorothy asked, her voice trembling.

"Aye," said the same woman, "I have."

"Oh, Aunt Lizzy," Dorothy said, sitting down, braving the bugs in the straw to be closer to Abigail and Aunt Elizabeth.

The woman laughed bitterly. "Child, I had little choice. Either I denied it and was hanged, or I confessed to it and was imprisoned for life. What choice is that?"

"Then the trials do not free one?" Dorothy asked.

Aunt Elizabeth put her arm around Dorothy. "'Tis true that no one has yet proven innocence to the magistrates. But there is always hope, niece, always hope."

"Hard to feel it here, though," another woman said softly.

"Aye," Aunt Elizabeth said. "One must work hard to maintain faith in this dismal place."

Abigail stared at the woman who had admitted to being a witch. She looked just like the others, dirty and haggard, but otherwise normal. Was she indeed innocent, as she claimed, or could it be possible that she was lying and was really a witch?

"Are there days when food does not come, Aunt Lizzy?" Dorothy asked.

"Nay, child," Aunt Elizabeth said. "In this cell, we are fed better than most. Our families have paid most dearly for our upkeep, so we are fed regularly and given this goodly sized cell. But I fear the food will leave you hungry. It is not much." She paused. "Still, 'tis better than what those whose families cannot afford their upkeep will receive. They get very little, and in the end, if they cannot pay the jailer his fee, they remain here until their debts are paid, innocent or not."

As if he had heard them speak, the jailer came down the steps a moment later, preceded by a light in the hallway. Two young boys followed him, each carrying wooden bowls steaming with something hot.

Abigail's mouth watered. Neither she nor Dorothy had had anything to eat since breakfast.

The jailer went down the rows of cells, doling out food to many. But he passed several others without stopping. Abigail heard the pleading of those who could not pay, crying for mercy and for more food. *It would be difficult to have an empty belly, to smell that food yet have none of it,* she thought.

At last the jailer reached their cell. The boys with him were breathing heavily from the hard climb up and down the stairs to fetch bowls of food.

"Move back, move back," the jailer called to the women who had been crowding the door. They moved swiftly away. The jailer took out his ring of keys and opened the cell door.

Abigail and Dorothy lined up with the others to receive their supper. Abigail was careful to leave some space between herself and the woman in front of her. In this place, there seemed to be no telling if one was next to a witch or not, and Abigail would not risk that closeness.

When she reached the head of the line, the jailer handed her a wooden bowl and a rough wooden spoon. Abigail glanced down. It was broth, with only a few small, stringy pieces of meat in it. If this was what she was being fed, what did those who did not pay as well get? The jailer handed her a piece of bread. Abigail took it, noticing the mold along one side of the slice.

"Please, sir," she said, "might I have another piece? This bread is moldy."

"If it's unhappy you are, then eat it not," the jailer growled, snatching away her bread. "Let the soup fill your belly tonight."

Abigail gasped with surprise at the abruptness of his gesture.

"Please sir," she said, realizing that she would go hungry if she did not eat some of the bread. "I am truly sorry. That piece will be fine."

"Please," Aunt Elizabeth said behind Dorothy, "'tis their first day here, and they are most hungry. The child is sorry she has offended you."

The jailer gave Aunt Elizabeth a sharp look, but then relented, handing Abigail back the moldy bread, which she took eagerly. Abigail understood now why Aunt Elizabeth had looked so frightened of their jailer. It was he who controlled their lives.

Dorothy was not so wise. She stared down at the clear broth and then handed it back. "Surely for what my Papa has paid there is more than this!" she said.

"Dorothy!" Aunt Elizabeth gasped.

Abigail turned and looked back at her sister. She prayed the jailer would not beat Dorothy for the comment, or do something even worse. Still, there was a part of her that admired her sister for having the courage to confront the jailer.

"Nay," the jailer cried, anger in his voice. "There is naught else, and with impertinence such as this, you shall not receive your candle that has been paid for either. Now move on. May your wicked, ungrateful little belly rumble loudly in your ears, for you'll get naught to eat from me on the morrow either."

"You can't do that," Dorothy protested.

"I can and I have," the jailer replied. "Now move on."

With that, he gave her a shove, pushing her toward the back of the cell. Dorothy stumbled in her heavy leg irons, but quickly righted herself and moved toward Aunt Elizabeth's bug-infested bed. Abigail and Aunt Elizabeth joined her there.

Dorothy looked disdainfully down at the plates in their hands. "I wouldn't eat that food if it were on real delft china," she said haughtily.

Aunt Elizabeth sighed. "You will be happy enough with this food after having had naught for two days, niece. That was truly a most foolish thing to do, and now that our jailer has withheld your tallow candle, I fear you will get little sleep, either."

"Why?" Dorothy asked. "Because of the condition of the bed?"

Aunt Elizabeth shook her head. "Nay," she said. "Because of the rats."

Then she bent to eat her food.

fifteen

"Rats?" Dorothy gasped.

Even Abigail felt sick thinking of those awful creatures. Though they rarely frightened her, she was not overly fond of them either.

"Aye," Aunt Elizabeth said. "They mostly come during the night. It would have been better had we three candles near our corner rather than two, since the candles keep them at a distance."

Dorothy lifted her legs and chains up onto the straw. It seemed she was willing to risk bug bites rather than face the rats.

When they had finished their meager meal, the bowls and spoons were collected by the jailer's young helpers. Then they were left again in the silence and darkness of the cell.

"Come. We must be about preparing for sleep," Aunt Elizabeth said.

"How do you even know when the nighttime comes?" Dorothy asked.

Aunt Elizabeth shrugged. "There is a rhythm to the day that you shall soon learn."

Abigail wondered why they should worry about sleep when it seemed as if nighttime were all that existed in this gloomy place. But she stood as her aunt asked her to do.

Aunt Elizabeth fluffed at the straw. "We will have to share this bed," she said, "but no matter. The closeness will keep us warm, as this place grows cold at night."

"Colder still?" Abigail asked in wonder, for even now, her feet and hands were raw and damp.

"I fear so, niece," Aunt Elizabeth said. "Come. Let us lie down and find a comfortable way to be together upon this bed."

Abigail and Dorothy removed their heavy leather shoes and stretched out upon the straw. Aunt Elizabeth joined them, lying at the opposite end of the wooden bed and spreading upon them all a thin blanket.

"Is this all there is to keep us warm tonight?" Dorothy asked.

"Be grateful, Dorothy," Aunt Elizabeth replied. "Most here can afford no cover at all."

Dorothy said nothing, but Abigail saw her pull the blanket up over her head, and then heard her sobbing. Abigail turned on her side and put an arm around her sister, drawing her close until Dorothy's body fit snugly against her own. She held her sister, comforting both of them, until at last, she felt Dorothy's body soften in sleep.

Abigail stared at the cell walls, on which the tallow candles made flickering shadows. She thought of home, of Franny and her dolls, of Paul and his gruff love, of Edward growing so fast, and of Mama and Papa. They seemed so far away now. The sound of her heart was loud in her ears, and her mouth was dry. Abigail knew herself to be a courageous girl, but she could feel the fear in this place like a rough cloth against her face, smothering her. She longed for the forgetfulness of sleep, but it would not come. Instead her head was filled with horrible images of waking to find a witch above her, and it was a long time before she finally fell into a fitful sleep.

． ． ．

Abigail woke in the middle of the night. The cell was quiet, except for the snoring and occasional murmurs of some of its occupants. Her back was cold against the wall, and she turned over to warm herself against Dorothy.

She knew that something other than the cold had awakened her. She listened and heard a slight scratching sound. Rats had come into the cell. Dorothy slept soundly beside her, and Abigail was grateful, for she knew her sister would have been horrified to hear them.

There was a slight movement at the end of the bed where her aunt slept. Aunt Elizabeth began to cough.

Abigail hoped she would stop and soon slide back into sleep, but Aunt Elizabeth's cough worsened, growing louder and louder. That must have been what had wakened her.

"Aunt Elizabeth?" Abigail finally said into the darkness.

"Abigail, I meant not to wake you."

"Do not worry, aunt. I fear the rats would have disturbed my sleep anyway."

"Well, child, go on back to sleep. It will give you strength, and you shall need that here."

"Are you not afraid that perhaps the witches in here will come for you as you sleep?" Abigail whispered.

"We are all chained, Abigail," Aunt Elizabeth said. "In truth, I have been here a month now and have suffered no torments at these women's hands."

Abigail thought about this, still wondering if some of them would not try to recruit her for the devil. Her aunt began coughing again.

"How long have you had your cough?"

"A fortnight, but it is naught. It comes only at night. Do not worry, Abigail. Sleep."

Aunt Elizabeth coughed again, her body shaking with the effort of it. Abigail listened to the force of the cough, aware of what it might mean.

"Is there blood?" Abigail asked when Aunt Elizabeth had stopped.

At first her aunt said nothing. Then, quietly, she replied with a sigh, "Aye."

Abigail moved her leg so that it touched her aunt's. "We need to get you out of here soon, then," she said, trying to keep her voice light and her concern hidden. Coughing blood was a serious sign, especially in a place so damp and cold.

"Please say naught of this to your mother," Aunt Elizabeth said. "I do not wish to frighten her and Daniel." She coughed again and then spoke softly. "Abigail, you are strong, and so I will speak truthfully to you. I hold out little hope for my trial. Not one has been found innocent without accusing another. If they refuse, they are condemned."

"Then you must accuse someone else, aunt," Abigail said.

In the dark, Abigail could sense Aunt Elizabeth smiling.

"And condemn another innocent to this most horrid of places?" her aunt asked. "Come, Abigail. Surely you do not mean me to do this?"

Abigail knew it was not right, but if her aunt was not freed from here, Abby knew death would be a possibility. But then, her aunt must realize it too.

"Nay, Aunt Elizabeth," she finally said, steadying her voice. "Nay, I would not have you lie."

"Good child," Aunt Elizabeth said. "Let me say just one more thing, then. Though release for me seems unlikely, I cannot believe that the magistrates will hold two such as Dorothy and you. Your young age will surely convince them of your innocence. As for me, in spite of what has happened to the others, I am still determined to survive, if for no other reason then to hold my dear Daniel in my arms once more. This desire, I believe, will give me strength to find an answer as to how to effect my freedom, Abigail. Now let us both turn our minds to sleep."

Abigail did as her aunt asked and fell silent. But sleep would not come for her. That night she listened to the rats and her aunt's cough and prayed for an answer to save them all.

The food brought them in the morning was no better than the evening's meal. But Dorothy, on waking hungry, was quick to beg forgiveness of the jailer. Though he grumbled and complained, at last he gave in and handed her a bowl of the awful grub. Still, Dorothy could not resist making a face before eating the horrible mush. Abigail was glad to see her sister eat, and gladder still to see that Aunt Elizabeth's cough had stopped.

When the meal was finished and removed, they were left again in the dim light with nothing to do for the rest of the day. The other women sat on their beds or on the floor and stared into the darkness. Abigail, too, sat in silence, and the longer she sat, the more she was certain she would not survive this place. She longed to cry out, to beat on someone, to wake up and find she had only been dreaming this nightmare. And though it seemed impossible to believe, she longed to have chores to do: mending, sewing, baking, weeding. She would have welcomed these things now to make the time go faster.

Just when she thought she would go mad from it all, a light appeared above, and the jailer descended with Mama behind him. Mama moved slowly, her belly large with the baby.

Relief flooded through Abigail at the sight of her mother. She would have a plan and news of what was being done to get them all released. Abby ran her fingers through her hair and tried to press down her dress. She wanted to look good for Mama.

"'Tis Mama," Dorothy said. "Let us move to the front of the cell so that she may not be aware of the chains on our feet."

"'Tis a good suggestion, Dorothy," Aunt Elizabeth said as she rose to greet her sister.

"Abigail and Dorothy Faulkner," the jailer said, "you have a visitor."

Abby smiled brightly. From the corner of her eye, she could see that Dorothy was doing the same, but Mama was not deceived. Her eyes fell on the chains, and she began to cry.

"Dear God," she whispered. "'Tis a far more horrid place than I had even imagined."

"We are fine, Mama," Dorothy said.

"We have eaten and slept well, Hannah. You mustn't worry," Aunt Elizabeth added.

Mama began pacing outside their cell, shaking her head back and forth. Abigail watched, her concern rising. This was not like Mama.

"How can I not worry?" Mama cried. "The house seems empty without you girls. We all miss you. You will understand when you have children of your own. If I do not free you soon, I will be destroyed. It is truly unbearable for me to see you like this."

Abigail had never heard her mother speak like this, as if she was out of control.

"How fares Papa?" Abigail asked, hoping to focus Mama's mind on other matters.

But it did not help. Mama gripped the bars of the cell so hard that her knuckles turned white.

"He began hearing voices again on his return," she said. "I tried to soothe him, but this morning the demons plagued him still. For once I could not help him, and I know not what to do to help you, either. I feel all is lost—everything I have loved and worked to keep together."

Abigail stared in fright. Her mother had always been the strong one, the one with a plan, the one who would aid them and comfort them. But now she seemed spent.

"Mama," Dorothy said, "you frighten me when you talk like this. Surely Grandpappy will find a way to free us. Do you not believe that the magistrates will find us innocent when they hear our case?"

Mama shook her head back and forth, saying nothing. Dorothy looked at Abigail, her eyes wide.

Then Abigail felt a hand on her shoulder. Aunt Elizabeth had moved to her side. The light the jailer had left fell full on her thin body and tired face. But when she spoke, there was no weakness there. "Hannah! You do these girls and the baby you carry no service in such an emotional state. Pull yourself together, sister, and concentrate your energies on your family and the means to free your daughters."

Mama looked up. Her eyes widened as she saw Elizabeth in the light.

"Eliza," she whispered, "you look most horrible."

Aunt Elizabeth let out a laugh. "Thank you, Hannah. You do not look particularly well yourself. But come. We were both aware of the horrors of this place before I or the girls arrived. I will watch over them here and keep them safe. But you, my dear sister, must do your part, too."

Mama shook her head. "What?" she cried. "What is there for me to do?"

"Hannah," Aunt Elizabeth said sharply, "I know not. I am in here, but you are there. You must find a way to convince these magistrates to free your daughters. There has to be a way, Hannah, and for them, you have to stay strong and find it."

Mama stared at the floor.

"The Lord will help you, Hannah," Aunt Elizabeth said.

Mama laughed bitterly. "The Lord has deserted us."

Aunt Elizabeth shook her head. "Nay, sister. Our fellow man has deserted us. God is still with us, and he will save us. I believe that. And sister, if I can believe that, being *here,* surely you can believe it as you return home."

Mama lifted her eyes to Aunt Elizabeth's. They looked at each other for a long time. Then, slowly, Mama nodded. "Aye, sister. You are right."

She sighed. "Forgive me, girls. I have been consumed with my own suffering. Aunt Elizabeth is right. You shall not be free unless I fight for your freedom, and this I promise to do. Though it pains me to see you, I must forget this heartache and work toward a solution that will end all our troubles."

Tears streamed down Dorothy's cheeks.

"I must go now, girls," Mama said, "but I will find a way to free you. On this you may depend."

Telling them that she would be back in two days, Mama called for the jailer and was led away. But Abigail did not feel better. With Papa ill and Mama herself pregnant, what strength could she find to help them to freedom? Abigail looked back at the darkened cell.

She would give anything, say anything, to be out of here. But what? What could she do that would convince the magistrates she was truly innocent?

sixteen

Abigail and Dorothy settled

into the routine of Salem Town Prison. August gave
way to September and then October, with no break
from the cold, dampness, or dull weariness. Abigail's
arms and legs were soon covered with red sores from
the bedbugs. Her hair grew greasy and full of lice.
Her eyes burned from the smoke of the tallow candles,
and she was no longer able to distinguish the bad
smells of her cell. She knew that she, too, must smell
as awful as the others around her.

As the weeks passed, Dorothy seemed to give up
all hope. She did nothing all day but stare off into
the darkness. Many times she refused to eat, though
she took what was offered, only to sit on the bunk
with the food held listlessly in her lap.

Aunt Elizabeth's health worsened. Her cough, racking her only at night before, now continued into the day. Some days she never left her bunk, lying for hours with the heaving cough, which left her face spattered with blood.

As Abigail watched them worsen, she feared for her mind. She knew the time would come when, like Dorothy, she would have no courage to get up at all, but would sit half-mad next to her sister, staring out into the darkness, not caring anymore.

Mama and Uncle Daniel came every other day to visit. They brought knitted caps from Franny, a whittled animal from Paul, and new stories of Edward's escapades. But their visits did little to lift Abigail's spirits. Though Uncle Daniel was hopeful with Aunt Elizabeth, Mama grew more depressed with each visit. Papa had worsened, rarely leaving his bed now, muttering over and over that someone was after him. Mama had tried hiring help to watch him, but each one lasted only a day or two before their fear of Papa's fits and witchcraft led them to believe that Papa was afflicted by his own daughters, who were able to reach him from their cells.

This rumor, reported in guarded tones by Uncle

Daniel to Aunt Elizabeth, but overheard by Abigail, worried her. If the magistrates learned of this tale, they could have her sentenced before she was even able to plead her case.

It seemed to Abigail that their lives could not possibly get worse. Then came the rains.

In that terribly dark and gloomy place, Abigail was not aware of the fact that fall rains were coming down heavily outside. It wasn't until she noticed a wetness along the base of the floor that she learned of it.

"Aunt Elizabeth," Abigail said, pointing, "what is that?"

Elizabeth turned her pale face toward the seams of the floor of their cell. "I know not," she replied in a puzzled voice.

"Ah, no," a voice moaned, "'tis the fall rains from outside. They must have saturated the ground. Let us pray that the rain ceases, for if it does not, the seawater will begin to rise."

"Inside the cell?" Abigail asked.

"Aye," another voice said. "'Tis what happens so close to the ocean. The floor of this cell will not hold it back. I daresay we will be walking in saltwater before the week is out."

Abigail prayed for the rains to stop. Their conditions were terrible enough without having the jail cell flooded.

But the next morning, the water continued to press its way inside, and the morning after, an inch covered the floor.

"Up, up you go," the jailer called out. "I'll not be bringing your food in to you like a servant. If it's food you want, you must come to the door to get it."

Abigail rose with the others and gingerly made her way to the line for food. Saltwater seeped into her shoes and stung her feet with cold. Abigail looked at the hefty boots on the jailer's feet and envied him. She would remember to ask Mama to bring them all boots when she was next here.

"Abigail," Dorothy whispered, "I cannot seem to get warm."

Abigail put her arm about her sister. "If I could get your supper for you and let you return to bed I would, but you know he will not allow it."

"I can manage," Dorothy said. "But I fear Aunt Elizabeth may not fare as well."

"Aye," Abigail agreed, turning to see Aunt Elizabeth in line behind them, her body trembling from the cold water. "But we will do what we can. Tonight we will draw close to her, and try our best to warm her."

But that night, Aunt Elizabeth would not hear of it. "Nay," she said, coughing heavily and trying desperately to draw a breath. "I can manage at this end nicely. Curl yourselves together, girls. You need the warmth more than I."

Abigail opened her mouth to object, but she knew it would do no good. Aunt Elizabeth was stubborn and would not hear of them warming her if it meant either one of them would be cold. So Abby drew herself to Dorothy and held her close that night.

Early the next morning when Abigail awoke, she sensed something was wrong even before she saw that there were things floating in the now ankle-deep water.

"What is that?" she asked.

"'Tis rats!" someone cried.

Dorothy sat up beside her, looking down into the water of their cell. "Abigail," she moaned, "what are we to do? Is it not bad enough we are bothered by these demons at night? Must we suffer their presence during the day, too? How shall we go for our food?"

"You can't really think he'll come down here to feed us with these rats about?" a woman laughed. "Nay, girl. We will go hungry until the waters go away."

"Oh, Abigail," Dorothy moaned, "how shall we survive without food?"

But Abigail did not answer. Though everyone was awake and staring in horror at the rats swimming about their cell, one person had not moved. Abigail felt underneath the thin blanket for Aunt Elizabeth's leg and shook it gently. Her aunt did not move, and her leg was cold.

Abigail looked at her sister, tears tumbling from her eyes.

"Dorothy," Abigail whispered, "our aunt is dead."

seventeen

Dorothy scrambled to move away from the dead body. She stared at her aunt, who lay motionless beneath the thin blanket.

"Abby," she whispered, "what are we to do?"

Abby wiped at her tears. "There is naught we can do now, Dorothy," she said.

Abby looked at the white face of their aunt, so pale and gaunt in death. She remembered the day her aunt had wed her uncle, how happy they had both been on that day. Abby had been only four then, but she could still see their smiling faces in her mind. Now Uncle Daniel must face a life without Aunt Elizabeth. Abby bent her head and wept for Uncle Daniel, for her mother, who must now face life without her sister, and for her grandfather, who had lost one of his daughters. Aunt Elizabeth had been but twenty-four. How quickly her life had passed, only to end here, in this miserable prison. What if tomorrow Abby should start coughing? Would *her* death be swift? Would she end her days here in this horrid place?

The other women in the cell sat upon their beds, staring at the girls and their dead aunt. They said nothing to comfort them.

But Dorothy, who was sitting on the other side of Abby, suddenly pushed past her and waded into the rat-infested water.

"Dorothy," Abigail said, rising to her knees, "what are you doing?"

"Hello!" Dorothy yelled out into the dark. "Hello, up there!"

There was no response.

"Do you hear me?" Dorothy yelled again. "Hello! We need help down here!"

"You'll get no answer," one of the women muttered.

"Well, I've got to try, haven't I?" Dorothy said, whirling on the women, facing them defiantly. A rat swam next to her. Dorothy shot out her leg and gave it a good, swift kick. She turned back to the bars of the cell.

"Hello!" she screamed. "Help! Help!"

To Abigail's amazement, a door opened above.

"What's the commotion all about down there?" the jailer yelled. "People are trying to sleep. If you don't pipe down, I'll not feed you, not a one of you, you hear?"

"Please, sir," Dorothy cried out, "my aunt has passed away. Please. Won't you send for my family?"

There was a silence from above.

"What's the family, then?" the jailer finally called down.

"The Faulkner family, sir," Dorothy answered him.

"Fine. Fine," the jailer said slowly. "I'll send on word. But no more noise or I might change my mind. Understood?"

"Yes, sir," Dorothy called out.

The door closed, and Dorothy waded her way back to the bed. Abigail looked at her with new appreciation.

"That was very brave of you, Dorothy," she said, putting her arms around her sister and hugging her tightly.

"'Tis nothing," Dorothy said. "Come, Abby, for now we must be braver still."

"You mean because now we are alone?" Abigail asked.

Dorothy shook her head. "Nay, sister," she said. "Because we must be about preparing the body of our aunt."

For the first time in her life, Abigail took direction from her elder sister. In all the years that she could remember, she had been the brave one. But Aunt Elizabeth's death seemed to have given Dorothy a courage she had not shown before.

Dorothy pulled back the blanket and found Aunt Elizabeth covered in her own blood. "Abigail," Dorothy instructed, "rip a piece off your undergarments and dip it in the water below. We must clean her as best we can."

Abby did as she was told, tearing off a piece of her petticoat. As she bent over the water, the rats swam near, thinking she had food. She shooed them away and dipped the cloth in the water. Then, with Dorothy helping, she cleaned the blood from Aunt

Elizabeth's face and neck. There was little they could do about her gown.

Abigail shivered when she felt how cold a body turned once its spirit was no longer there. She wished to turn away from the gruesome task, but Dorothy's determination kept her focused. If her sister could do this, then so must she.

"Hand me your comb, Abby," Dorothy said.

Again, Abigail did as her sister commanded, and Dorothy scrambled up onto the far side of the bed, carefully lifting Aunt Elizabeth's head into her lap. Slowly, she began to comb out her hair. When the knots were all worked out, she arranged the hair, skillfully plaiting it and curling it on top of Aunt Elizabeth's head.

At last she crawled back down and carefully placed Aunt Elizabeth's hands over her chest. Abigail looked at their aunt. She was white, almost alabaster, and her skin had shrunk into itself about her cheeks. But at least now she looked presentable and peaceful.

Abigail laid her head against her sister's shoulder. "That was truly a brave thing to do, Dorothy," she whispered.

But her sister was crying now, and Abby realized that Dorothy's newfound courage had been but a temporary thing. She hugged her sister close, taking back the role she had grown up in all her life.

The jailer would not come to the cell when he saw the amount of water on the floor. But he did keep his word and sent home news of Aunt Elizabeth's death. It was the next day when Mama, Uncle Daniel, Grandpappy, and Paul arrived. Abigail felt a great weight lift from her shoulders when she saw them coming down the stairs. Last night, she had kept herself away from her aunt's body, but several times had wakened to feel her aunt's cold leg next to her own. It had shocked her each time.

The jailer led her family to the cell and opened the door, grumbling the whole time about the water. The rats swam from the unwelcome light of the jailer's torch, as he lifted the blanket from Aunt Elizabeth's feet and unchained her. Uncle Daniel was the next one in. Without seeming to notice the water, he knelt next to Elizabeth and placed a hand on her forehead. Then he laid his head on her chest.

Mama came and hugged Dorothy and Abigail.

She looked down at the face of her sister. "Did you girls arrange my sister so?" she asked.

"'Twas Dorothy's idea, Mama," Abigail said.

Mama nodded. "I can see it was truly done with love, girls," she said. "Thank you."

Grandpappy came in too, and kissed Abigail and Dorothy. He looked over at his daughter, lying still upon their bed. "How many more lives will be lost in this madness?" he asked.

Abigail did not answer. What could she say to his question?

"You'll need to hurry there," the jailer growled. "I must get this door closed so them witches don't escape."

"In good time," Grandpappy said. "We've paid to retrieve the body."

"Shall be in *my* time," the jailer retorted, "or I'll have my boys carry her out and bury her in a pauper's grave as all the others who've not been retrieved by their families."

Grandpappy's eyes flashed with fire. "You speak to a man of the cloth," he said angrily. "Mind your tongue, or it shall be a day in the stocks for you."

The jailer scowled but was quiet.

Paul came into the cell. He shrank from the other prisoners, his eyes turning to Abigail.

"They'll not hurt you," she said, going to his side. "We're all chained."

"Oh, Abby," he said, looking about him. "I hate to think of you and Dorothy in this place. I hate not being able to help you get out of here."

"Help Mama," Abigail said.

"Aye," Paul agreed. "You know I will. Papa has had fits more frequently these days. I think the fear for you and Dorothy has been too much for him."

Grandpappy pulled Abigail and Dorothy to him. "Let us pray for your aunt's goodly soul," he said.

Mama, Paul, Abigail, and Dorothy bowed their heads while Grandpappy said his prayer. The women around them bent their heads too, and for once, they were together as one.

When he had finished, Grandpappy went over to Uncle Daniel and laid a hand on his shoulder. "Come," he said. "Let us be about taking my daughter from this horrid place."

Daniel nodded and stood.

"Here boy," Grandpappy said, turning to Paul. "Lend us a hand."

Paul nodded and went forward. He reached under Elizabeth's waist and lifted, while Uncle Daniel held her head and Grandpappy lifted her feet.

"Come along, come along," the jailer groused, having found his voice again and deciding to risk the minister's wrath. "I have other chores to attend to."

Mama turned an angry face to the jailer, but Dorothy laid a hand on her mother's arm. "Mama," she said softly, "do not forget who decides our fate in this place."

Mama swallowed hard, then nodded. Uncle Daniel, Grandpappy, and Paul carried Aunt Elizabeth to the cell door.

"Be strong, girls," Grandpappy said. "Your mother and I will find a way to get you out of here."

Uncle Daniel said nothing, but Paul's sad eyes met Abby's. Then they were gone.

"Ma'am," the jailer said, indicating that Mama should leave.

"Papa is ill?" Abigail asked quickly, wishing to prolong the visit.

Mama nodded. "Aye. He is distraught," she said.

"I could not let him come and see Elizabeth here. I asked him to stay with Franny and Edward and told him he must be about finding a spot in which to lay my sister to rest."

"We shall not be there," Dorothy said softly.

"She would know that you meant to be, child," Mama said.

She hugged and kissed them both. Then she followed the jailer up the long prison stairs, the light disappearing with them.

The other women turned away from Abigail. Their moment of togetherness had ended. Abby stared into the dark at their now empty bed.

eighteen

In the stillness of that morning,

Abigail lost all hope. Like her sister had before, she began sitting day after day, caring little if she ate or if she starved. She stared out at the darkness, her mind numb, no longer longing for freedom, ignoring the awful truth of Aunt Elizabeth's death. For the first time in her life, all she could feel was fright. Every little thing scared her. Every little noise made her jump. She was going to die. She knew it.

She retreated and spoke not at all, simply closing her mind off. It was not until many days later, when Mama stood directly in front of her, shaking her hard, that Abigail even became aware of the fact that her mother was there.

"Abigail!" Mama cried. "Abigail, rouse yourself, daughter. Do not frighten me so."

Abigail stared at her mother. She wondered why Mama was screaming. Could she not see that there was no hope? Could she not feel the end and the frightfulness of it?

"Abigail," Mama cried again, putting her arm around her and rubbing her shoulders.

"Here, here, Mistress. Not so close. 'Tis not permitted. I could have trouble for letting you into the cell as it is," said the jailer.

"Can you not see that she is ill?" Mama snapped.

The jailer glared at her but said nothing more.

"Abigail," Mama said, her voice dropping to a whisper. "Bear, I know this has been a hard time for you. But I have good news! Good news! I have the way to free you at last!"

Into Abigail's vision came the face of her sister. "'Tis true, Abigail," Dorothy said. "Mama has devised a plan whereby we shall be quit of this place. Think on it, Abigail! Free from this horrid prison! Free from this cell of death! Come, Abby. Listen to Mama. We must do as she tells us."

Abigail looked at them both. What good was freedom if Aunt Elizabeth was not here to have it also? Or was she free? Did her spirit roam about now, glad to be rid of this earthly hell? Abigail shivered.

The slap, when it came, was hard and shook Abigail to the core. "Rouse yourself, daughter," Mama scolded her. "They may have taken Elizabeth, but they shall not take you also. It is time to fight, Abigail. I mean to bring you home."

Home, Abigail thought. *Home.* Somewhere deep inside her something stirred, a hope, a glimmer of her old self. Could it be so? Could she be rescued from this horrible cell? Could she return to someplace warm, somewhere safe?

Abigail opened her mouth for the first time in days. Her voice cracked from lack of use. "How, Mama?" she asked. "How can I get home?"

Mama smiled. "I have managed to arrange your trial for the day after the morrow," she said.

Abigail's heart fell. The fright returned. "What of it?" she croaked bitterly. "The trial offers little hope."

"'Tis true if you refuse to accuse someone as your teacher in the devil's ways," Mama said, her eyes glowing and dancing with some secret.

"Would you have me falsely accuse someone?" Abigail asked, crying. "Would you have me condemn someone to this life?"

Mama nodded, smiling again. "Aye, Bear. I would."

"Who?" Abigail cried. "Who would you have me name as a witch, Mama, that I might go free?"

Mama hugged Abigail tight. "Me, Bear," she whispered. "You will accuse me."

nineteen

"Nay, Mama!" Abigail cried, suddenly thinking clearly. "Are you mad?"

Mama shook her head. "I am not mad, Bear," she said. "This seems to be the answer. If an accused witch accuses someone else of teaching them the devil's work, the accused is considered innocent and is freed. The teacher of the devil's ways is then arrested in their place."

"Surely, Mama, you are aware that they will arrest *you* then, and *you* will be imprisoned in this place," Abigail said.

"Aye. I know this to be true," Mama said. "But at last I shall have some peace, knowing you and Dorothy are to be safe."

"And when your trial comes," Abigail said

scornfully, "will you in turn accuse someone, or will you refuse to confess to being a witch and thus be condemned to death?"

"That is our secret," Dorothy said. "Mama will refuse to admit to being a witch, but they cannot condemn her."

"And why not?" Abigail demanded. "They have hanged many for their refusal to speak."

Mama smiled and rubbed her belly. "They may not hang one who is with child," she whispered. "So you see, I am saved."

What Mama said was true. Witches who would not confess but who were with child were not hanged until after the birth of the baby. But did this make things right?

"What if we are unable to free you after the babe is born?" Abigail said. "What if you should sicken here and die like Aunt Elizabeth?"

Dorothy's eyes widened. "I had not thought of this, Mama," she said. "What if we cannot free you after the babe is born? What then?"

Mama rubbed Dorothy's head. "I will be fine, Dorothy. I am strong. This you know, and the babe will keep me safe. Even now there is talk of protest against those doing the accusing. Grandpappy speaks out against it daily. 'Tis only a matter of time before reason returns, and the babe will give us that time."

Abigail stared at her mother. Did she truly believe they could go through with this? What her mother was asking was too much! How could she possibly stand in front of the magistrates and accuse her own mother of teaching her witchcraft? And how could she condemn her to this horrible place?

"Nay, Mama," Abigail said. "I cannot do it."

Mama's hand dropped from Dorothy's head. She stood, drawing herself up tall in front of Abigail. "You will do it, Abigail Faulkner. You will do it because I am telling you to."

Never had her mother spoken to her this way. Then her mother's face softened, and tears came to her eyes.

"You will do it because I can take the thought of you here no more. My torment does but hurt the babe inside. Truly I say to you, Bear, you must do this for me so that I might rest easy," Mama said.

She went to the cell door and called for the jailer. Then she turned once more to her daughters.

"Over the next day, talk to each other and prepare stories for the magistrates," she said. "Say the stories together, for they must sound true should they ask. Now I must go, for there is much to do to prepare for my coming absence at home."

The jailer opened the door.

Mama smiled slightly. "At last," she sighed, "at last, you will be set free."

Then Mama was gone, and Abigail and Dorothy stared at each other. Abigail's fright had been replaced by the horror of what they must do. If Mama was right, and Dorothy and Abigail played their parts, they would be free in two days' time. But how was Abby to live with herself after she had accused her own mother of witchcraft?

The day of their trial, Abigail and Dorothy were led from their cell. No one wished them luck nor said good-bye, but Abigail was not surprised. Friendships in places full of suspicion were not easy to make.

Still, when the leg irons were taken off her feet, she turned one last time to look at the bunk on which she had rested with Aunt Elizabeth. Though she did not believe in ghosts, there was a part of her that wondered if some spirit of Aunt Elizabeth's still wandered these halls, unsettled and angry.

"Come," the jailer grumbled. "Or perhaps you'd prefer to stay a little longer?"

Abigail quickly shook her head and with her sister followed the jailer down the darkened corridor and up the stone stairs to light and freedom.

When they reached the top, Dorothy put a hand to her eyes. Abigail, too, shut her eyes, for the sunlight hurt after being in darkness for so long.

They were led to a small room in the prison where Mama waited for them with a tub of steaming water. Mama helped them take off their clothes and bathe. She combed their hair to free it from nits and lice and helped them dress again in clean clothes, all the while hugging them to her and planting kisses on them. Her happiness was overwhelming, and whenever Abigail or Dorothy started to protest what they were about to do, Mama would hush them.

"Free. You are *free,* girls," Mama said, smiling through her tears. "You are clean and in fresh air once more. Do not break my heart now with talk of refusing to do what I have told you to. Nothing, no jail, no cold, no hunger will affect me as much as seeing you in this place did. Now my heart sings at your release."

"We are not released yet, Mama," Dorothy reminded her, "and if we are, it will be at the price of your freedom."

"Aye, daughter," Mama said, laying her cheek on Dorothy's freshly brushed hair. "But if you do as I have told you, 'tis only a matter of time, and we will all be free."

Dorothy looked over at Abigail, and Abby knew her sister mistrusted those words as much as she did.

When at last they were clean and presentable, Mama came with them outside. Abigail felt like a young child, for the sights before her seemed fresh and new as if she had never seen them before. She breathed in the sea air and watched the people bustling about. Autumn was in full swing in New England. The trees shone in all their colors and brilliance, and there was a crispness to everything. In front of her lay the ocean, sparkling in the October sunshine. Vessels lay at anchor, rocking peacefully back and forth on their moorings.

Freedom, Abigail thought. *But at what cost?*

She forced herself to put the thought from her mind and climb up into the prison wagon to begin the journey to the meetinghouse. She was weak from her stay and welcomed the ride.

Dorothy looked at her and smiled. For a moment, Abigail pretended they were only out for a day in town, riding in the autumn sunshine with not a care in the world.

But when at last the Salem Town meetinghouse came into view and she saw the crowds outside awaiting her trial, she shook herself free of that dream. Today would be one of the most difficult days of her life.

The wagon came to a stop, and Grandpappy came around to the back. A constable lifted first Dorothy and then Abigail to the ground. Grandpappy hugged them both. As he pulled Abigail toward him, his lips brushed her cheek. "Thank the Lord you have agreed to this plan of your mother's," he whispered. "Though I fear it might be ill advised, I know that she must be at peace knowing you are free. Without that, she will surely die from worry."

Abigail looked into her grandfather's eyes. He seemed older than she remembered, and she knew that the past months had taken their toll on them all. Would any of them, accused and accusers alike, ever be the same again?

"'Tis still a lie, Grandpappy," she said to him.

Grandpappy nodded, his eyes clouded with worry. "Aye, granddaughter," he said. "But one that I think the Lord will forgive."

"Will he?" Abigail asked.

Grandpappy lowered his eyes to the ground and when at last he looked at her again, there were tears in his eyes. "I am an old man, Abigail. I have lost a daughter to this madness, and it may be yet that I will lose another. Should I lose you and Dorothy, also? Nay, I think not, child. The Lord will understand that perhaps this was but a means to stop a madness. Do as your mother tells you, Abigail. End her pain."

"And what of my pain, Grandpappy?" Abigail asked.

Grandpappy drew her near him, and she waited for his answer. But this time the man of the pulpit had nothing to say.

171

The constable came to them and touched Abigail on the shoulder, telling her to come into the meeting-house with Dorothy. Abigail drew a deep breath and went up the stairs, mustering her courage as best she could. Yet she felt faint, and her stomach sickened as she took those first steps toward condemning her mother.

twenty

The meetinghouse was filled with people who had come to see Dorothy and Abigail and their trial. Many of the people were from Andover, yet there were others who were unfamiliar to Abigail. She wondered what could have brought them from their chores and their fields to watch the trial of two total strangers. The constable led them to the front and told them to sit on a pew. Dorothy's hand slipped inside Abigail's, and Abigail gave her a squeeze though her own palms were damp.

A few pews back, Abigail saw Grandpappy, Mama, and Papa. Paul, Franny, and Edward had stayed at home. They had wanted to come, but Mama had refused to let them see what was to happen.

Papa's face looked drawn and tired. He smiled when Abby looked his way, and Abby was puzzled by that smile. Did he know what they were going to do today or had he been too sick lately to be told of the plan? Was it even wise to have brought him here?

"I did not expect so many," Dorothy whispered.

"Aye," Abigail agreed, looking again at the packed meetinghouse. "It is most unusual that strangers would care what becomes of us."

"Mama says there have been a great many at each trial," Dorothy said. "She says that most of Salem Town attends, and that their fields lay fallow. She fears many will starve come winter for having neglected their duties to attend these trials."

"'Tis no concern of ours, Dorothy," Abigail said sharply. "Truthfully, I do hope they all starve for showing such ghoulish interest in our case."

Dorothy smiled. "'Tis exactly what Mama said. Still, Abby, I am most fearful of today," Dorothy continued. "I pray our words are enough to convince them to free us, and yet, I cannot truly believe that in speaking them we must condemn Mama."

Abigail touched her forehead to Dorothy's. There seemed little to say to this.

The constable was coming down the aisle again, and at his side was Sarah Phelps.

"Oh, there is that most hateful Sarah," Dorothy said. "I truly wish I could scratch her eyes out, for she has been the cause of all our pain."

Abigail was inclined to agree with her sister. Still, as she looked around the room at the faces full of fear and hatred, she could not bear to continue all the mistrust that seemed to surround them.

"Forgive her, Dorothy," Abigail said, surprising herself. "She was but frightened by something she did not understand."

"You sound like Grandpappy," Dorothy said, "but if it was not for her, we would not be here."

"Aye, but what is done is done. Let us work to end this madness, not prolong it."

"Still, I shall hate her," Dorothy said.

Abigail nodded. She understood. In her mind, Abigail knew they should forgive Sarah, but she could not prevent her heart from feeling hatred too.

There was a commotion outside, and at last, the three magistrates entered the meetinghouse. They were severe-looking men in black wool coats and dark hats, their faces stern and unsmiling. They walked to the front of the meetinghouse and sat down behind a large table.

Then one of them stood. "Today we are to hear the case of Abigail and Dorothy Faulkner. We will start with a prayer to our Lord."

Abigail lowered her head but no prayer came to her lips. She could think of nothing today to be grateful for. She had already prayed for release a million times before without an answer.

"Amen," the magistrate said. "Let us begin the trial of Abigail and Dorothy Faulkner with the testimony of the tormented one. Come forward and state your name."

Sarah Phelps walked slowly forward to the front of the courtroom. She held her hands stiffly at her side, and when she spoke, her voice shook.

"Speak your name, girl," the head magistrate commanded, "and give us a full account of your tribulations at the hands of these girls."

Meekly, Sarah nodded. "My name is Sarah Phelps, and I do live in Andover. I did most recently work for the Faulkners. They were kindly to me, and yet Master Faulkner did often have fits which were most horrible to see. I had made up my mind to end my employment there when I did see Mistress Faulkner, who was ill at the time, sit up in her bed and scream out as if someone had sat upon her bed. Then I did see Abigail and Dorothy Faulkner go to her and soothe her."

A murmur rose from the crowd.

"She was but with fever!" Dorothy cried out, unable to stop herself.

"Hold your tongue!" one of the magistrates warned her. "You will have your time to speak."

Sarah glanced uneasily at them, then quickly looked away.

"Continue," the head magistrate commanded.

"I did run from the house then," Sarah Phelps said. "But Abigail Faulkner followed me. She turned on me an evil eye so that my throat did close, and I could not speak for a fortnight."

Abigail stared at Sarah. How could she say such a thing? Abigail remembered casting an angry glance at Sarah as she ran to find Papa, but that had been out of irritation at her leaving them, not a devil's eye.

Sarah caught her looking and threw up her hands. "Nay," she cried. "Nay, please do not look at me so.

I fear she is casting her evil eye on me even now."

A murmur went up from the crowd. Abigail was shocked. Surely it was not evil to cast an angry look at someone who was falsely accusing you? And yet, maybe now it *was* considered evil. Abigail dropped her eyes.

"The accused is not looking upon you now," a third magistrate said, his voice soft and kind. "Have you more?"

"Aye," Sarah Phelps said. Abigail's head shot up. What more could there be?

"When I returned home, I lay without speaking upon my bed," Sarah said, "and for six days did Abigail and Dorothy visit me."

Visit her?

"What is she talking about?" Dorothy muttered to Abigail.

Abigail shrugged. She had no idea. They had not seen her again after that day.

"They flew about me in the night," Sarah said, "begging me to join them and do the work of the devil. They told me they would continue to torment me unless I did as they ordered. But I refused. Once my voice returned, I did go and accuse them."

Abigail's mouth dropped open. Was Sarah mad? What was she talking about?

Abigail turned to look at the townspeople. They were staring at her in horror, in total belief that she and Dorothy had done this. How were they to prove that they had not flown at Sarah and threatened her?

"Sister," Dorothy said softly, "we are undone."

In that moment, Abigail understood. There *was* no way to prove you were innocent. If the magistrates allowed Sarah to claim such a thing to begin with, then they had already lost. Their case was decided.

For Abigail and her sister, and for the others who had gone before them, there were only three choices. Deny it all and condemn yourself to hang, because you would be unable to prove the accusations untrue. Speak, and admit to being a witch, and return to prison. Or speak and say that you were following another's instructions, and in accusing someone else, free yourself. This, Abigail saw, was what Mama wanted. Mama had known there were only these three choices, and that Abigail and Dorothy would not have the ability to use reason as a weapon. Here in Salem Town, reason was not present.

"Rightly done," the head magistrate commended Sarah. "Tormenting witches must be brought to justice. I thank you, Sarah Phelps, for your efforts on this community's behalf."

Sarah nodded and sat.

The magistrates turned their stern faces toward Dorothy and Abigail.

"Rise, Abigail and Dorothy Faulkner," the head magistrate said. "What have you to say to these accusations?"

Dorothy's hand still clung to Abby's. She turned her eyes toward Abigail. Abigail looked back over her shoulder.

Mama was staring at her, nodding, urging them to go forward and condemn her. Grandpappy was across the aisle from her, holding Papa's hand, as if he could give his own strength to Papa, who had none.

"Well?" the head magistrate's voice boomed out. "Are you to speak, Abigail and Dorothy Faulkner? If so, rise and do so."

"Aye," Dorothy said softly, rising as she spoke. Her voice shook with fright. "I will speak."

Here she hesitated.

"Yes," the magistrate prompted.

"I am not a witch," Dorothy whispered, "but have only been following the instructions of my mother, who has been dealing with the devil."

With this, Dorothy slid back into her seat. Behind her, the townsfolk screamed and shouted, and they moved away from Mama as if she had smallpox.

"Aye," Sarah Phelps shouted. "Dorothy is right. 'Tis not they who are witches but the mother."

"Quiet!" the head magistrate shouted into the screaming crowd. "Quiet!"

He turned toward Sarah. "How are you come upon this conclusion?"

Sarah stood, her face eager. "'Tis the mother who does have the power to calm Master Faulkner from his fits, and 'tis the mother who did see someone upon her bed. Who could it be but the devil?"

Again, the meetinghouse grew loud with voices.

"Quiet! Quiet!" the head magistrate shouted out again.

Then he turned toward Abigail, his face stern. "You have said naught. What say you to this charge? Was it indeed your mother who told you to torment Sarah Phelps?" He waved his quill pen at her. "Come, child. Speak. What have you to say?"

twenty-one

Abigail looked back at Mama,

whose eyes begged her to speak. She looked at Dorothy and saw shame in her sister's face. Abigail's heart went out to her older sister.

"Come, child," another magistrate said. "Speak and tell us if what has been said is the truth. Has your mother told you to do the work of the devil?"

Abigail still said nothing. She could not believe this was the answer to ending such madness, but on the other hand, she couldn't leave her sister alone to do this terrible thing.

"Speak, Abigail Faulkner," the head magistrate said. "Tell us if you are falsely accused."

Abigail looked back at her mother again.

"Speak," Mama mouthed to her.

Abigail buried her face in her hands. Oh, how she longed to be out of this place. How she wished for the matter to be settled some other way! What was she to do?

"Speak, child," the head magistrate's voice boomed out.

"Please, Abigail," Dorothy whispered. "Do not leave me alone to do this. I could not live if it was only I who condemned our mother."

"Speak, Abigail Faulkner," Grandpappy called out. "End your suffering, child."

"Speak, child!" another magistrate shouted. "Answer us! Did your mother instruct you in the devil's ways?"

"Speak out!" cried another voice.

"Speak! Speak! Speak!" The voices of all in the meetinghouse sang out at her. They rang in her ears without mercy, drowning out the voices in her own head. They overwhelmed her with their loudness until she could stand it no longer.

"Aye!" Abigail screamed, silencing them all. "Aye, my mother did tell me to do this."

The meetinghouse erupted. Abigail fell to the pew in a slump, unable to control her sobbing any longer. *There*, she thought, *I have done it. Yet I didn't lie. Mama* did *order me to stand here today and do this.* Dorothy put an arm around Abby's shoulders and bent her head toward her sister's. She, too, was crying.

"Arrest that woman!" the head magistrate called out.

Abigail turned to watch, tears streaming down her cheeks.

Constables appeared. Mama rose with all dignity and put out her hands so that they could be tied together. Her chin was high, her eyes steady. She looked at Abigail and Dorothy, and she smiled. But Abigail could see the slight fear in her mother's eyes.

Across the aisle, Papa had risen too, his face clouded with confusion. Grandpappy put his hand on Papa to steady him and keep him from following Mama.

"'Tis the most horrid thing I have ever done, Abby," Dorothy whispered. "I can only remind myself that they cannot put Mama to death. The babe will save her. Oh, Abby, did we do the right thing?"

"I know not," Abigail replied. She wondered how her mother, pregnant, would be able to handle the cold and damp cell better than they could at the ages of ten and twelve. Abigail thought of Aunt

Elizabeth, dead in her grave. Would Mama die too?

"Abigail and Dorothy Faulkner," the head magistrate's voice boomed out.

Abigail turned with her sister to face that formidable man.

"You are free to go. The court does thank you for your honesty in helping to prevent the spread of witchcraft in our colony."

Honesty? Abigail thought.

Mama was led up beside them. She was shaking slightly.

"Hannah Faulkner, I do commit you to Salem Town Prison until such time when you may be heard on these accusations," the head magistrate said.

"What is happening?" Papa's voice was loud in the meetinghouse. "Where do they take Hannah?"

Abigail looked back at him. Grandpappy whispered to Papa, finally telling him, it seemed, of their plan. Abigail saw his eyes grow wide, and he slumped down into the pew, staring at Mama as if she had betrayed him.

The others in the meetinghouse stood looking with hatred and fear at Mama. Fear and hatred. Jealousy and anger. That was what all this was about.

Lies and more lies. And today Abigail Faulkner had had a hand in continuing the river of madness. She who had withstood the stocks. She who had braved the rats and the cold of the prison cell. She had given in to fear today. She was no better than Papa.

Or was she? In the end, who was to decide what she should do? Was it these people? Was it Mama? Or was it she who was responsible for her actions? Wasn't it *she* who should decide?

So what was it to be? Was she to be the girl who had given up in a mean, damp prison cell after her aunt's death, or the girl who had defied them all, lifted her skirts high, and raced with pleasure?

Papa was praying in his pew. But he did not try to stop them from taking Mama. They began to lead Mama away, and he did nothing.

In that moment, it became clear to Abigail who she was. She was not and would never be her father. No one would make her decisions. She would not be bound up with fear. She was her mother's child. Today and every day, she would do as *she* decided. She stood and cried out into the room.

"Nay! Stop! I must speak!"

Mama turned, her face white.

Abigail felt her mother's pain, but so too did she feel her own. The meetinghouse was quiet.

"I have not been honest with this court and the magistrates," Abigail said.

Mama moaned.

Abigail looked back and saw Grandpappy grip the back of his pew. Papa's head came up. The meetinghouse erupted with noise again.

"Quiet!" the head magistrate shouted. "What is this, child?" he said. "What are you saying?"

Abigail swallowed hard, then stepped forward with determination.

"Sir," she began, "it is not true that my mother did teach us witchcraft. My mother is no witch. Nor am I. Nor is my sister."

She thought back to the women in her cell, the women she had avoided as if they had plague. She saw them there, in the darkness, in the cold and damp, each struggling in her own way to survive the madness that had befallen them. And she saw her aunt. She knew Aunt Elizabeth would urge her to speak, to speak the truth, her truth as she knew it to be and with the strength she had always had.

"There are no witches here in this courtroom,"

Abigail spoke out. "There are no witches in all of Massachusetts, nor in all the land."

The whole of the meetinghouse seemed to gasp for breath.

"You must end this madness," Abigail said, looking right at the magistrates. "You must listen to reason. Sarah Phelps has claimed that I did fly about her. How is she to prove this? If she cannot prove it, and yet you convict on her words only, who is to say that next you will not be accused? Each and every one of you?"

"But we are innocent," cried one woman.

"As am I," Abigail rejoined, turning now to the crowd. "But there is no way for me to prove this to you, as you are set to believe something that Sarah Phelps simply says."

Abigail sighed, looking back at the magistrates. "Please. Can you truly believe that witches have been your neighbors for these goodly years and you did not know it? I beg you. End this madness now. Release those in prison."

A great quiet came to the meetinghouse. Abigail waited. Would the magistrates listen to her? Would they see reason?

"But then," one voice from the crowd said quietly, "how do you explain the behavior of the Salem Village girls?"

"Aye," another voice called out. "You must explain how they came to be tormented."

Abigail's heart sickened. They did not believe her.

Then Dorothy stepped to her side and took Abigail's hand.

Abigail felt her strength return. "The girls are lying," Abigail said quietly. "They have been play-acting."

"Nay," a voice called out, "I believe her not. She does but confuse us to save her mother. The mother is instructing her to say these things. Take the mother away, and the daughter will be free of her powers."

"Aye," Sarah Phelps said, jumping up. "Aye. 'Tis she who is the witch. Why even now I can see the mother's spirit flying about our heads. Oh, look! Look! Do you not see her?"

All eyes turned to where Sarah Phelps had pointed. There was nothing there, but the people were shrieking and covering their heads as if her mother's spirit flew at them.

"Abigail Faulkner," the head magistrate intoned, "for lying to this court that your mother was no witch, you will spend a day in the stocks on the morrow. Take the mother away now. Free the daughter from her powers and leave her to think on her lies."

twenty-two

A great despair fell over Abigail. She had failed. Dorothy dropped her hand and slumped to the floor, but Abigail ran to her mother.

"I am sorry, Mama," Abby whispered. "I did try to lie for you, and yet I could not."

"I should not have asked you to," Mama said. "I see that now. But Abigail, rest easy. You did try to right a wrong, and though the crowd turned against you, you did what you knew to be right and true. I am proud of you, Bear."

"I will keep trying to end this thing, Mama." Abigail promised.

"As will I from my cell," Mama said. "Yet I shall

rest easy knowing you and Dorothy are well and at home. Keep Papa safe for me, and give my love to your sister and brothers."

She kissed the top of Abigail's head.

Dorothy came up to them, and Mama kissed her, too.

"I am sorry, Mama," Dorothy said, crying.

"It was what I told you to do, was it not?" Mama said, smiling. "Do not worry, Dorothy. Take care of things for me at home now and know that I love you."

A constable began to lead Mama outside, and she stumbled slightly on a step as she walked. Dorothy turned away, but Abigail followed Mama out of the meetinghouse.

I have failed, she thought as the wagon pulled up for Mama. *What I did was for nothing.*

Abby watched as Papa hurried to embrace Mama. She saw him shaking as her mother whispered words of encouragement to him. She had done no better than Papa in stopping this from happening.

Grandpappy came and stood beside Abigail, but he said nothing.

Mama was helped into the wagon. "I love you,

Bear," she cried out. "Stay brave, and bring me news when you have it."

"Aye, Mama," Abigail yelled back.

As the wagon pulled away, Abigail could see that her mother was crying at last. She watched until the wagon turned a corner and was gone. Papa stood in the middle of the road, unmoving, as if he were a lost child.

"You were brave to speak out, Abigail," Grandpappy said softly. "It could have cost you your life had they chosen to believe you for a witch."

"And what would it have cost me, Grandpappy, had I said nothing?" Abigail asked.

Grandpappy nodded. "Quite a bit, I suspect. And for knowing that, I know you for the good soul that you are, Abigail."

"A good soul does little for me, Grandpappy," Abby said bitterly. "Do you not see that my speaking out has had no effect? I might as well have stayed as silent as Papa. I did fail."

"Did you?" a voice said.

Abigail looked up. There stood an unfamiliar man.

"Governor," Grandpappy said, standing straighter, surprise in his eyes.

"I was most affected by your speech today, Abigail," the governor said. "I believe that you spoke the truth."

Abigail stared at him.

The governor smiled, a sad smile. "They have accused my own wife, Abigail. I have taken her safely away, but I came back to see to the accusation against her. Listening to you today, I know what must be done. I intend to join your grandfather and end this madness."

Slowly, Abigail's spirits began to lift. Maybe there was hope for Mama after all. Maybe speaking out in the midst of madness had done some good.

"Truly you mean it, sir?" she asked.

"Truly I mean it, Abigail," he said. "For your mother's sake, but also for my wife's."

Papa came up the stairs slowly, shaking his head from side to side.

"What am I to do without her?" he said softly. "How am I to survive?"

"You must be strong, Papa," Abigail said impatiently.

He looked her in the eye. "Aye, Abby," he said. "I know this to be true. I am weak, though I do truly try to be different. Why can I not be strong and courageous?" he asked, his eyes imploring Abby to answer. "Why must I be plagued by these fears that torment me, by these voices in my head?" He looked away. "Why can I not be more like you?" he whispered. "More like your mother?"

There was such pain in his voice. Standing there, Abigail saw her father as if for the first time. He was not like other fathers. He never had been. But for once, Abigail understood how much that pained him. Never once in all her years had he admitted to her that he was aware of his illness, that he wished for things to be different. *What must that be like?* Abby wondered.

For a moment, she thought back to the days right after Aunt Elizabeth's death. She had been afraid then, unable to fight anymore. Abby realized that she had had a glimpse of the fear that consumed her father. Could she truly hate him for something he could not control, when he wanted nothing more than to be rid of it?

She put her arm around her father. She had been

blessed with strength. He had been cursed with weakness. Who was she to condemn him for this? He might not be the strongest of fathers, but perhaps he did try harder than most. When he was well, Papa was kind, and Mama loved him much.

"Come," she said. "Let us go home."

Dorothy was standing in the doorway of the meetinghouse. "Home," she said. "Truly, Abigail, have you ever heard a better word?"

Abby smiled. "Nay, sister. I have not."

"Let us be about it, then," Grandpappy said.

twenty-three

When Abigail's house came into sight, she began to shake. It was as if a part of her had doubted this could truly happen. And she knew that until Mama was home and safe, fear was to be her companion, just as it was for Papa. It was a strange and unsettling feeling.

As the wagon drew near, the door to the house flew open. Franny was in the doorway, waving wildly. She had Edward in her arms. Abigail could see Paul running in from the fields, Uncle Daniel with him. Never had Abigail been so happy to see her family.

Abigail hugged Dorothy to her. They had made it. They were home.

When the wagon came to a stop, Dorothy

scrambled out and ran to Franny. Abigail jumped down after her. She took Edward from Franny and planted kisses all over him. He had grown so big while they were gone. He squirmed and bucked until she let him go. He stared at her suspiciously.

"Edward, it is me, Abby," she said, hurt by his behavior.

"He has not seen you in three months, Abigail," Papa said softly. "That is a long time for a fellow his age."

"Papa," Edward said, lifting his chubby arms high into the air and running for his father. "Papa. Papa. Papa. Papa. Papa."

Papa swung Edward high, and he let out a belly laugh.

"He talks!" Dorothy cried.

Grandpappy chuckled. "Too much if you ask me."

Abigail went over to Franny. "You haven't changed too, have you, little one?"

"I think I grew a bit," Franny said hopefully.

"I do not want you to change, Franny," Abigail said, hugging her sister. "I want you to stay just as you are."

"But I must grow, Abby," Franny said impatiently,

"or I will never be big like you and Dorothy."

Abigail thought of all the things she had endured the past few months. Growing up was no easy task.

"Are you all right, then, Abby?" Franny asked, her eyes wide. "Did the witches in the prison torment you?"

"Nay," Abigail said softly. "There are no witches there, Franny. Only poor souls as confused as Dorothy and I were."

"And Mama?" Franny asked.

"She will be safe there," Dorothy assured her.

"And we will get her back, Franny," Abigail added. "I promise."

Paul came huffing and puffing into the yard. "'Bout time you two came back. Lollygagging in Salem Town while I'm left with all the harvesting and fall chores."

Abigail grinned at him "'Tis glad I will be of chores, Paul."

"Mayhap you need some time in Salem Town Prison to consider the good fortune you have in doing your chores, Paul," Grandpappy said gruffly.

It was meant to be a joke, but immediately everyone grew silent. Abby could think only of Mama, now imprisoned in that dark and dank place. And when she saw Uncle Daniel, she could no longer see her own homecoming as a happy occasion. Her uncle seemed to have aged overnight. There were lines around his eyes and mouth, and his hair had begun to gray.

"Uncle Daniel," Abigail said, going to him and hugging him close.

"Thank God you are all right, Abby," he said, hugging her back. His voice cracked when he spoke.

Dorothy came and hugged him too. "Can you show us where she's buried?" Dorothy asked.

Uncle Daniel nodded.

Aunt Elizabeth's grave was easy to spot. The grass had just begun to grow over the black dirt mound. They stood together as a family, yet it felt incomplete with Mama missing.

"Aunt Elizabeth was a great comfort to us, Uncle Daniel," Dorothy said.

Uncle Daniel nodded. "She was a great comfort to me, too, Dorothy."

A cool wind blew through the trees, making Abigail shiver. Yet, looking around, she decided that the spot where Aunt Elizabeth was buried was a good one. There was a fine view across the fields, and the trees behind them would give good shade in the summer.

"You chose well, Papa," she said, remembering that Mama had left that task to him.

"I looked a goodly time," Papa said softly, and then sighed. "If only it had not been necessary."

"'Twas a waste," Paul agreed.

"Her life was not a waste, Paul," Grandpappy said. "It may have been short, but it was a life filled with love."

Uncle Daniel nodded.

"Come," Grandpappy said. "It is late, and we must see to supper."

Franny skipped on ahead with Grandpappy and Uncle Daniel. Dorothy hooked her arm with Papa's as he carried Edward toward home. Abigail hung back until she was alone with Paul.

"I'm glad you are back," Paul said gruffly.

"As am I," Abby said.

"If only Mama hadn't had to . . ." Paul's voice trailed off. He looked out over the fields and the stone walls.

"She didn't have to, Paul," Abigail said. "She

chose to. It was a sacrifice she wanted to make."

He kicked at the dirt with the toe of his shoe. "Makes me angry, though," he said. "I can think of nothing to do to help her. I feel as weak as Papa."

Abigail knew that feeling of resentment. She thought about these last weeks, the fear she had felt then and now. She hated it, and yet it had taken hold of her. Fear, she had learned, was hard to shake.

"He tries to fight it, Paul," she said.

"Since when have you taken his side?" Paul asked.

"Are there sides?" Abigail shook her head. "Nay, brother. I have seen too much division and distrust in jail and at the trial. Let it not break up this family, too. This has been a terrible time, and yet in some ways I know good has come of it."

"Good?" Paul looked at her in surprise.

Abby nodded. "I learned something during those days in prison and at the trial. Each of us is trying the best we can, Papa especially. He cannot help the illness that plagues him, just as I cannot help the color of my hair or the shape of my face. But I am not him. Nor are you. Fear may come to us, but you and I can beat these fears. Truly I think so, Paul."

She smiled at her brother. "We are too strong to

be frightened forever. No one can ever tell us what we should say or how we should think."

She thought of Elder Stevens that day of the race and the look of disapproval on his face. "No one."

Paul gave her a rueful smile. "You look most formidable when you speak this way, Abby. Remind me never to anger you."

She gave a short laugh. "I think that may be an impossibility. You know my anger is quick."

Paul nodded, serious again. "But usually right."

"There are things we can do to help Mama," she said, putting her arm around her brother. "I know not what they are yet, but I am determined to find a way to free her."

Abigail looked at the sun, setting now across the fields, at the colors in the trees, and at her home in the distance. She dropped her arm from her brother's side, lifted her skirts, and tossed her head defiantly.

"Race you," she challenged him.

Without waiting for his response, Abigail flew across the fields. She could hear her brother running hard behind her. But he would not beat her. No one could.

author's note

In the fall of 1987 I was living in Andover, Massachusetts. I had grown up in Pittsburgh, Pennsylvania, where my mother's family had been for generations. My father's side of the family was German and had settled in St. Louis, Missouri, and Alton, Illinois. I didn't think I had any connection whatsoever with the East Coast.

So it was a great surprise when I was told by my father that we had ancestors who had arrived on the Mayflower. Another branch of my family was of Puritan stock, and members of that family were accused of witchcraft, convicted, and jailed during the Salem witch trials in 1692.

I was fascinated. My father came to visit, and

together we began to research our family's Puritan roots, learning of my great-great-great-great-great-great-great-great-great-grandfather Reverend Dane and my great-great-great-great-great-great-great-grandmother Abigail Faulkner. As we pored over old documents and books, some amazing facts emerged. Not only had my ancestors been involved in the witch trials, but they had lived in the very town I was living in at the time of my father's discovery. Beyond that, they had owned the very land on which my own house stood!

The connection was too spooky for me to ignore. I felt a calling to write a book about them. For me, the most intriguing aspect of all was this: Why did Abigail Faulkner turn upon her own mother, saying that she had recruited her to work with the devil?

Then one day I looked at my own two daughters, and I knew. Her mother had told her to do it. By accusing her, Abigail went free, and her mother took her place in Salem Town's prison. What parent would not do this for a beloved child? And so I wrote *The Sacrifice*.

Although the story of the Salem witch trials has been told often, few are aware how deeply towns other than Salem Town (now Salem, Massachusetts) and Salem Village (now Danvers, Massachusetts) were affected. At one point, Justice Bradstreet refused to sign any more warrants in Andover, because so many had already been issued. In fact, more people were accused in Andover than in any other town, including Salem Village itself!

The Faulkners were a family caught up in the upheaval. Both Abigail and Dorothy were arrested and imprisoned, as was their aunt, Elizabeth Johnson. Elizabeth Johnson did not die in prison as she does in my novel, although due to the deplorable conditions, many of the accused did.

Here are some other facts I changed for the sake of the story:

Abigail's mother's name was also Abigail. I renamed her Hannah.

Paul's real name was Francis. I renamed him to avoid confusion as well. Paul was actually the eighth child in the Faulkner family, born after the Salem witch period.

The Faulkner family had six children at the time of the trials, not five. In addition to Dorothy, Abigail, Francis, Franny, and Edward, there was an older sister, Elizabeth. Later, Ammi and Paul were born.

Aunt Elizabeth had two children, Hannah and Steven. They were also imprisoned, but they were released after their trial.

Abigail's mother was accused of witchcraft before her children were, and she was in prison with them for a short time. I left this aspect out, as I wanted her free to worry about her children. It is true that Dorothy and Abigail accused their mother at their trial, and that they were freed as a result.

These facts are also true:

Records show that Francis Faulkner did have "fits," and it was reported that only his wife was able to soothe him. There are reports that the fits caused him to suffer memory loss. Madness was not uncommon during that time. Chores and religion were the sole occupations of the day. There was no time for play, for children or for adults. This monotonous existence led many people to suffer mental illness. In fact, it is speculated that hysterical depression may be what the original accusers suffered from.

Abigail's grandfather was in fact the minister of Andover, and he did try to speak out against the hysteria that consumed the town. He was ignored as the fury spread. After Abigail's mother was convicted based on Abigail's and Dorothy's accusations, Reverend Dane and several others took a petition to the governor of Massachusetts to try and free her. Abigail's father was suffering from his illness again and did not go on the trip. He did, however, sign his name to the petition, drawing a heart pierced by an arrow beside his signature.

Abigail's mother did go on trial, and she is described as having been "a lady" in her denials. She was found guilty but was spared hanging due to her pregnancy. The trial was packed, as most of the trials were, and it is true that when the hysteria ended, many townsfolk starved, having neglected their fields and crops in order to attend the trials.

In the end, when the governor ordered the witch trials to cease because his own wife had been accused, Abigail's mother was given a reprieve. Three months later, she bore a son. She named him Ammi Ruhamah. The biblical name means "My people have obtained mercy." Perhaps she named him to express her relief that the witch hysteria was finally over and her family was, at last, free. I like to think so.

bibliography

Brown, David C. *A Guide to the Salem Witchcraft Hysteria of 1692*. Worcester, MA: Mercantile Printing Company, 1989.

Hill, Frances. *A Delusion of Satan: The Full Story of the Salem Witch Trials*. New York: Da Capo Press, 1997.

Karlsen, Carol F. *The Devil in the Shape of a Woman: Witchcraft in Colonial New England*. New York: Vintage Books, 1989.

Mofford, Juliet H., ed. *Cry "Witch": The Salem Witchcraft Trials—1692*. Carlisle, MA: Discovery Enterprises, Ltd., 1995.

Starkey, Marion L. *The Devil in Massachusetts: A Modern Enquiry into the Salem Witch Trials*. New York: Anchor Books, 1989.